laurel
everywhere

laurel

everywhere

ERIN MOYNIHAN

Laurel Everywhere
© 2020 Erin Moynihan

ISBN13: 978-1-947845-19-0

Ooligan Press
Portland State University
Post Office Box 751, Portland, Oregon 97207
503.725.9748
ooligan@ooliganpress.pdx.edu
www.ooliganpress.pdx.edu
Library of Congress Cataloging-in-Publication Data

Names: Moynihan, Erin, 1996- author.
Title: Laurel everywhere / Erin Moynihan.
Description: Portland, Oregon : Ooligan Press, Portland State University, [2020] | Audience: Ages 12-18. | Audience: Grades 10-12. | Summary: After the death of her mother and siblings, fifteen-year-old Laurel Summers' father struggles with grief and depression, leaving it to her friends to help her cope with her pain and loss.
Identifiers: LCCN 2020013091 (print) | LCCN 2020013092 (ebook) | ISBN 9781947845190 (paperback) | ISBN 9781947845206 (ebook)
Subjects: CYAC: Grief-Fiction. | Fathers and daughters-Fiction. | Best friends-Fiction. | Friendship-Fiction. | Depression, Mental-Fiction. | Grandparents-Fiction.
Classification: LCC PZ7.1.M73 Lau 2020 (print) | LCC PZ7.1.M73 (ebook) | DDC [Fic]--dc23
LC record available at https://lccn.loc.gov/2020013091
LC ebook record available at https://lccn.loc.gov/2020013092

Cover design by Kendra Ferguson
Interior design by Morgan Ramsey
References to website URLs were accurate at the time of writing. Neither the author nor Ooligan Press is responsible for URLs that have changed or expired since the manuscript was prepared.
Printed in the United States of America

This one is for my family, both given and chosen.

1

Hanna is the one who finds me.

Hanna, with her soft brown eyes and perfect olive skin and voice that sounds both frantic and calming at the same time. I'm lucky Hanna is a worrier and Lyssa is usually lost or getting kidnapped (it happened once). I'm also lucky Hanna made the two of us turn on Find My Friends a few years back. I told her Dad was taking me on a hike and she asked where and I didn't respond. Then hours passed and her worry got the best of her.

She finds me in a laurel bush, with leaves framing my face and the smell of early-summer raindrops surrounding me. We're somewhere east of Seattle—I remember Dad getting on the highway. I remember the city disappearing behind us and the mountains and trees appearing as the highway seemed to expand, lane after lane.

I'm somewhere near Snoqualmie Pass, I guess. I'm not sure if Hanna can see the irony of it all (she looks too frantic to even recognize that it's a laurel bush)—not many people other than my mom regularly identify plants, but if anyone could, it would be Hanna. Hanna is a walking encyclopedia.

"Your face," she says. I wipe my hand across my cheek and feel blood, as if the branches dared me to a duel, and I just sat there taking the punches. She grabs my hand and holds on so tightly her blood pumps against mine—pumping the life back into me. I'm being reborn from the bushes: a family-less Laurel Summers with raindrops on her forehead and dirt on her cheeks.

Two weeks ago I would have laughed if anyone told me the predicament I'd end up in. But in two weeks, I've gone from being part of a family of five to being part of a family of only two; I planned a funeral, and now I've gotten left behind in my namesake bush.

My first thought should be Dad. He's not here. I'm not sure where he's gone. Hanna looks worried and her mom is here too, standing a few feet away with the same expression on her face. A mirror image of Hanna herself, except with lighter skin and blonde hair. But my first thought isn't Dad because maybe I'm not a very good daughter and in general not a very good person. Dad is all I have left and I should be looking for him, but instead my heart is melting and breaking into a million pieces because Hanna is holding my hand so tightly. I don't want to let go because if I do, all the life she's pumped back into me might spill out and I'll end up a de-flated balloon in the dirt.

"Where's your dad?" Hanna asks me.

I open my mouth but the words don't come out, which makes me wonder how long I've been underneath this bush, because my throat is dry and my lips feel like they're glued to-gether. It's still light outside, so at least there's that—the sun peeking through the rain clouds from earlier today. Instead of answering her, I point up the trail in the direction where I remember him stumbling away from me.

"You take her back to the car," says Mrs. Jackson to Hanna. "I'll look farther up. Hanna, call your father and tell him to get some people up here to search." Hanna's dad is a policeman. Hanna hates that he's a policeman because she thinks the justice system is messed up, but Mr. Jackson says he became a policeman because he wanted to be a good one

and show boys with dark skin like him they can become po-
licemen too.

Hanna puts her arm around me and doesn't even flinch when
my damp clothes touch her dry ones. She composes a short message to Lyssa: "Found her. She's fine." The fact that they're talking
about me sprouts a warmth inside my chest. It's nice to feel worried for sometimes, and it's especially nice to think Hanna was
paying attention to me and tracking my location. Even though it's
mostly because my family just died and I'm a loose cannon, lost
in the woods near the pass on a trail to some unknown destination that nobody but Dad seems to know.

A loose cannon. That's how I'd describe myself at the funeral. Dad cried the whole time: a steady, controlled flow of
tears. I didn't cry until the very end when they started a slide-
show and I saw this one picture of Rowan, Tansy, and me. I
realized I was the only one left alive in that picture and the re-
alization made tears explode from my eyes. Hanna and Lyssa
practically had to hold me down so I wouldn't run away. Dad
didn't look at me; I don't think he could bear it. If he'd seen
me, he would've burst into tears too. Together, we would have
drowned the whole funeral home—maybe the whole neighborhood—with so many tears even our rainy city of Seattle
would be swallowed whole.

That was the last time I saw Hanna and Lyssa, as they
were wrestling me down at the funeral. It was like the time
in seventh grade when Daphne Peters threatened to report
Lyssa for bringing alcohol to school and I nearly punched her
in the face to stop her. Lyssa and Hanna held me back and
lectured me about how if I'd punched her, we would've gotten
into even more trouble, and how she was just talking herself
up and didn't really want to tell anyways. The funeral was like
that, but much, much sadder.

Daphne Peters never did tell on Lyssa. I'd like to take
credit for that because I scared her with my menacing

twelve-year-old fist-swinging. (I'm not violent, I swear. Only when people are mean to my friends.)

Except at the funeral when they were wrestling me, I didn't have anyone in front of me to punch. I wanted to punch the guy who was driving the truck but why would he dare be at the funeral? He probably can't sleep at night. I can't sleep at night. I wonder what the man who drove that truck looks like. I wonder if he feels bad about it all or if he couldn't care less. I imagine him as a villain, large and intimidating, laughing in my face and at my mom's little car, broken and smashed to pieces while his giant truck remained intact.

We slide into the backseat of Mrs. Jackson's car. Hanna dusts off my pants and grabs my hands to stop them from shaking. The sun shines in through the windows and warms me up. Normally I'd be excited at the first sign of the season truly transitioning to summer, but instead I can't stop shivering. My hands won't stop shaking. They've been shaking almost nonstop for the past week, so I think it might just be one of those things that comes intertwined with death that nobody warns you about.

Hanna's hands are warm against mine. Before the funeral, we hadn't really spoken for a few weeks. She says it's because she was busy, but I know it's because we kissed and things got messy between us. But then my family died and I guess that made us forget about everything else, at least for a bit.

"I'm gonna call my dad," she says.

"OK."

Her voice sounds like it's underwater. Like I can hear it but I can't totally understand what she's trying to say. She hands me a half-empty water bottle while she talks to her dad on the phone. I chug the water and it burns against my throat, which tells me I was lying underneath the laurel bush for longer than I thought. Long enough to become parched and for the sun to move across the sky.

"My dad is on his way," she says. Hanna often talks to fill awkward silence, but lately she's been running out of things to say to me. I stare out the window at the trees and shrubs surrounding the trailhead. Laurel bushes are scattered all over the ground. They're everywhere. They make my chest tighten and a lump rise up in my throat.

"OK."

She hesitates before asking, "Where—where do you think your dad went?"

I don't know the answer. There's a voice in my head that tells me he probably flung himself from the mountaintop, and another voice wonders if he was mauled by a bear. Yet another wonders why in the world Dad would leave me lying there in my namesake bush all alone.

He'd suggested we go hiking. The two of us hadn't left the house in a few days and he'd said, "Why don't we go on an adventure?" I should have known then. He sounded far too chipper to be serious, but I hopped into the car and went along with it anyways.

I mean, he did take us hiking. We pulled over at an unmarked trail and before I even zipped up my jacket, he was powering up the hill. "Laurel bushes," he kept saying, pointing to the ground every time we passed a bush. "Look Laurel, you're everywhere."

I said something like "*They're* everywhere," and we both knew I wasn't talking about bushes. Mom was always the one who loved to point out our namesake flowers. Mom was a gardener, and she named us after flowers because of course she did. Rowan, Laurel, and Tansy.

Now: just Laurel.

After I said and thought all of that, my legs turned wobbly and I needed to rest. I lay down in a laurel bush and listened to Dad's footsteps slowly disappear into the distance. I thought he would come back for me.

He didn't.

Dad and I were always close. Mom and I were close too. I didn't have a favorite. I lapped up Mom's stories about astrology and herbal supplements and listened to Dad drone on about the difficulty of teaching English courses to freshmen who aren't majoring in English.

But now that Dad left me alone in a laurel bush, Mom should probably be my favorite.

I didn't have a favorite sibling either. Tansy and I would play games in the backyard, and I went to Rowan's soccer games and cheered for him with all my heart. I've always been neutral in matters of family. Mom said it was because I am a Pisces. "You're agreeable. You feel for others." Mom blamed most of our actions on our star charts, like the time Rowan got caught hooking up with a girl in a school janitor closet and Mom blamed it on him being a wild Gemini rather than the fact that he was an idiot.

Maybe it's too soon to call my dead brother an idiot, but he was. I didn't—don't—have a favorite sibling but objectively I can say Rowan is the least agreeable of the three of us. Was—is—I don't know.

"We'll take you back to your house," Hanna says, filling the silence again. "I can see if Lyssa wants to come over. Or do you want to come to my house? We can do that too. That might be better. And then my mom can feed all three of us and we can watch old TV shows on Netflix."

I don't say anything and she decides that we're going to her house. I would've picked that anyways, even if her voice didn't sound underwater and I had the ability to speak again. Despite chugging the remains of the water bottle, my throat is still on fire.

"I'll ask Lyssa to come over. Do you want Lyssa to come over?"

I nod. Lyssa helps—she gets it. Her mom is dead and she doesn't know her dad because she's been in the foster system since she was ten. She just tells people both her parents are dead because it's easier than telling them that her dad was just really messed up. Right after the accident, Lyssa and Hanna came over. Hanna tried to help by cleaning the house, cooking food in the kitchen, and offering to help my dad with planning the funeral. Lyssa just sat on my bed and talked to me about things that weren't my dead family, like music and the most recent season of *The Bachelorette*. Both were helpful in their own ways, but Lyssa feels calmer and less frantic. It's less like she's trying so hard to help and more like she just helps by being there.

Mr. Jackson pulls up in his police car, jumps right out, and meets Mrs. Jackson at the trailhead. They talk for a few minutes and then he disappears into the woods alongside a few more men and women in uniform. Mrs. Jackson makes her way back to the car, without my dad.

Did he leave me? Would he leave me? My parents left me one time in a Walmart. Mom said it was because I was the quiet one. Tansy was a baby and so she was attached to my mom in a backpack and Rowan was always talking and making noise. I got lost among the aisles of games and art supplies, and I didn't even notice they'd left until Mom came frantically running around the corner and wrapped her arms around me. I sometimes wish she hadn't told me they left and hadn't made a big deal about it, because I often think about how they left me. I think about it a lot. If she'd just grabbed my hand and said, "Laurel, it's time to go," I would've had no idea they'd ever left.

Being left behind seems to be the plight of the middle child. Even without my brother and sister standing beside me, living and breathing and taking up space, I've still managed to be forgotten somewhere.

"John is looking for your dad," Mrs. Jackson says. Her voice is calm but underneath I can tell she's a storm. She sounds just like Hanna when Hanna tries to hide that she's afraid.

"Thanks for picking me up."

"You don't have to thank me, honey."

The trees pass by my window like we're in a race and they're trying to beat me home. The sun continues to dip, turning the sky above us dark. I should be back there in the woods, looking for Dad, but my legs are tired and my face is covered in cuts and scrapes. I feel as though I'm running low on gas, and if I stay and look for Dad, my engine might give out. Maybe it's already given out.

What if they don't find him? Or worse, what if they do and he's…I can't think about that. So, I watch the trees and I imagine how it would feel to get squished by a car and how I'm going to ask Tansy how it felt to die when I see her in heaven—if there is a heaven. I wouldn't ask Mom or Rowan because both of them would lie. They'd try to tell me it felt like falling asleep. But Tansy, she'd be honest with me.

The trees pass by the farther we get from wherever Dad disappeared to. My phone lights up with a message from Lyssa linking to a Tumblr post full of *Stranger Things* theories. Hanna's foot taps nervously against the floor of the car so loudly I can hear it over Mrs. Jackson's music. I breathe in the air and wonder if ghosts are following me around now. If I breathe hard enough maybe I'll consume them and I'll be able to hear Mom and Tansy and Rowan inside of me.

Mom always told us ghosts were real.

I grew up in a family full of redheads. Mom, Rowan, and Tansy all had bright red hair, and I wound up with Dad's mousy hair color, somewhere in between red and brown. Sometimes, when we took pictures, it looked like we were two separate families—Mom with Rowan and Tansy, and just me and Dad. Hanna tells me my hair looks red like my mom's in the sunshine, when the light hits it just right. I used to make a big deal when we took family photos and insisted we shine a light on my head so I looked like a true-born Summers, a real part of the family, and not some cousin on my dad's side.

When I was little, I loved my older brother's hair. I would play with it and I cried when he would get it cut because I wanted to braid it. When I read *Harry Potter* for the first time, I became convinced my family was magical, just like the Weasleys. And then I got older and realized that living with them was less like being a Weasley and more like just coexisting with them, like I was their pet owl.

And to make matters worse (for me), they all have summer birthdays—even Dad. The summer-born Summers: Dad and Rowan in June and Mom and Tansy in July. I'm a February child; sometimes I wonder if I should change my last name to Winters.

Even if I had Mom's bright hair, I would still be the odd one out in the family. Mom and Dad used to laugh about it. Mom would throw her arms around me and say, "You're not the odd one out, you're just the middle child." She had two brothers, one older and one younger. I can't imagine Mom not fitting in. She was always the one at redheaded family gatherings who made the room light up when she walked in, and she danced on tabletops with her floral skirt twirling around her.

She died wearing one of her floral skirts, a "bright yellow tansy-colored skirt," as she liked to say. By the time Dad and I identified her body, the skirt had turned brown with dirt and blood.

Storybooks are always about orphans, or kids with abandoned families. Every Disney movie, tons of children's books—maybe it's to make kids like me feel less alone, but I certainly don't feel like a Disney princess. I don't know what I feel like. I thought the weeks after Mom and Rowan and Tansy died would be about missing them. I didn't think I'd be missing my dad too.

Even though Dad's car is still parked at the bottom of the unmarked trail, I'm afraid I'll look out the window and see his car in pieces like Mom's—like how the chunks of blue paint and broken glass were littered all over the freeway. The thought makes me hold tight onto the door handle all the way to Hanna's house.

Hanna's house is big, much bigger than mine, with marble staircases and a large backyard. Her mom says we have free range of it, probably because she feels bad for me, but all I want is to lie down on a bed and let Hanna drape her warm fuzzy blanket over me.

"I'll make food for you two," Mrs. Jackson says. "Lyssa, too, if she's coming. Go on and get washed up, Laurel."

"I'm already here!" calls Lyssa. "I let myself in."

Lyssa is the kind of friend who requires that we tell her the garage code so she can randomly appear at our houses whenever she likes. Mrs. Jackson jumps a little when she hears Lyssa's voice, but then she shakes her head and returns to rummaging through the kitchen freezer. She's used to Lyssa by now.

Lyssa wraps her arms around me, her dark hair smelling strongly of lavender shampoo, and I hear Mrs. Jackson say, "I'll put some pizza in the oven." It makes me think of how Dad and I wanted pizza and Mom, Tansy, and Rowan wanted ice cream, so we took separate cars and then they never came back. If I'd never made such a fuss about wanting pizza, maybe it wouldn't have happened like that. Maybe the truck would have taken all five of us, or we'd all still be living and breathing and sitting around in my house playing board games. Hanna must read my mind, because she gives her mom a look and her mom says, "Or just start light. I'll make salad."

The three of us disappear into Hanna's bedroom and before I know it, Lyssa is running a comb through my hair, saying something about needing to get me cleaned up. "There are twigs in your hair, Laurel. Why the hell are there twigs in your hair?"

Dad left me. He left me lying down in a bush. Or maybe I left him. He kept walking and he looked upset, yet I didn't get up and run after him. Was I supposed to go after him? What kind of father leaves his daughter? What kind of daughter is supposed to look after her father?

It's like I've lost a limb, like I've lost all my limbs, and they're all lying on the floor in front of me turning rainbow colors and I don't even recognize them anymore. My own life is suddenly foreign to me.

"They're going to find him," Hanna murmurs. She's pacing. I want to take the brush from Lyssa's hands and throw it at Hanna's head because her pacing is making things much worse. Back and forth and back and forth—it's like watching the hands on a clock, ticking along, never stopping, moving while the world around me has been frozen since the moment that truck smashed into my mom's little car. Lyssa obviously senses this because as she begins twisting my hair into a braid, she puts the brush down far out of my reach.

"Hanna," Lyssa suggests. "Why don't you put something on Netflix?"

"Right." Hanna nods, making it clear that she's completely forgotten our plan of distraction. I don't blame her; Netflix feels devoid of all comfort, considering my dad is missing and my family is dead while I'm just sitting here safely in Hanna's house.

Hanna and I have a weird relationship, and it had become weirder up until my family died. Then the weirdness seemed to subside because that's what happens when tragedy strikes. You forget about all the things that don't matter as much, you stuff your feelings deep down, swallow your pride, and show up.

Before all of this, Hanna and I used to bicker like an old married couple all throughout middle school, to the extent that our friends joked that we were married and we called each other "wifey." It was all a joke because that's what kids do, because it's a joke if it's two girls. If Hanna was a boy, it would have been very different: nobody would have joked about it. Instead, they would have asked us, over and over again, "Are you two dating?" And maybe we would have confronted our feelings sooner. But instead, we let it be a joke, a running gag, until suddenly, it wasn't.

Then I started to feel things, maybe Hanna did too, and things changed between us. We stopped calling each other "wifey" and Hanna and Lyssa began to date boys. I felt like I was tiptoeing around my own feelings, afraid to voice them to anyone, until one night Hanna kissed me. She got upset afterward and cried, which scared me because I thought she was incapable of crying ("It's because she's a Capricorn," Mom would say). Hanna stopped talking to me for a few weeks and started dating some boy named Jason, though I think they broke up—it all got lost in translation when my family died.

Lyssa acts like she's oblivious to all the tension between me and Hanna, but I bet she knows more than she lets on. Lyssa's good at keeping secrets. She says it's because she's been in foster care half her life, because apparently that gives someone like Lyssa refined secret-keeping skills.

"We could watch *Parks and Rec* again, or start something new. I've been wanting to watch *The Crown*..." Lyssa kicks Hanna in the back and she turns around, nearly whipping us both in the face with her curly hair.

"What? I'm just asking what you guys want to watch on TV."

Lyssa's gaze burns a hole through me. "Laurel? You in there?"

I'm not. I'm really not. I swear I feel Ghost Tansy playing with my hair and I hear Ghost Rowan asking me what happened between me and Hanna, because he feels the tension in the air, maybe even sees the tension. I bet ghosts see things humans can't.

And Ghost Mom. Where is she? Is she with Dad? Or would she stay with me? Dad was her person, but I was her daughter, and Dad left me and so did Alive Mom, so I really hope Ghost Mom hasn't abandoned me too.

"Laurel."

Lyssa grabs me by the shoulders and shakes me. Hanna tells her to stop and sits down beside me, suddenly losing her cold façade and becoming softer. Soft Hanna: the Hanna that comes out when she sees that her friends are hurting. She stops talking for a few seconds and sits down next to me and puts her hand on my shoulder. It's weird how people can do that, how they can flip a switch inside of their brains and become a different version of themselves when they need to. I've never been able to figure that out, and trust me, I want to.

I want to try on different versions of Laurel. But…I've always been just Laurel. Rowan was Rowan, with his loud voice and his all-star athlete reputation, and Tansy was Tansy, with her giant smile and obsession with collecting colorful rocks. I always told myself I just had to wait until I moved out, until I was on my own and no longer shrouded by two of the largest personalities ever to exist—three if you count my mom. I used to think that when I moved out and went to college, I'd travel the world and invent a new version of myself without my family always around to tell me who to be. But now they're gone, and I'm more lost than ever.

"What are you thinking about?" Hanna asks. Her voice is calm now, instead of frantic and silence-filling.

I decide that it's kind of pointless to lie to my best friends, so I say, "Ghosts."

Hanna's hand tightens on my shoulder and Lyssa laughs—two very opposite reactions.

"Lyssa!"

"Oh, come on."

I'm not sure why—maybe it's the sound of Lyssa's laugh and Hanna's offended "Lyssa!"—but I start laughing too. It all feels really familiar and I can practically taste the way things used to be between all three of us, before the accident, before the messy feelings, back when we were kids.

"I have a Ouija board," Lyssa says. Her eyes light up. Lyssa and Mom used to get along well—they'd talk about astrology and ghosts and crystals into the late hours of the night while Hanna and I eventually fell asleep in our sleeping bags, waiting for Lyssa to join us upstairs. Lyssa doesn't have a lot of her own things because she moves around a lot (all within the same school district, thankfully), yet of the few things she owns, one of her most treasured objects is a Ouija board.

"No," Hanna says. "No, no, nope. That stuff freaks me out. I know it's not real, but it freaks me out. Besides, my mother would have a heart attack if she knew we were inviting "spirits" into the house."

"It is *totally* real!"

"Have you ever seen a ghost?"

"Yup."

"In real life. Not on television."

"Well, no."

"Exactly."

Even though I've never seen a ghost before today, I feel Ghost Tansy leaning her head against my shoulder and I see Ghost Rowan shaking his head at me, laughing at the silly games I play with my friends.

"Laurel? What do you think?" Lyssa smiles at me and bats her eyes.

"I say that for Hanna's sake we can play with the Ouija board on our own, a different day."

Lyssa scoffs and Hanna mouths, "Thank you." Hanna's weird about ghosts and paranormal stuff. She says it's because she doesn't believe in it, but she has a cousin who claims he was possessed. The Jacksons wrote him off as crazy but I think Hanna believes him. Also, her mom is super Catholic and even though Hanna isn't, that whole Catholic-guilt stuff runs deep.

"Promise me," Lyssa demands.

"Sure."

"I'm going to make you go with me to an abandoned house. Or just the woods. We'll summon spirits there."

"Great."

"You know," Hanna mutters, "This probably isn't the best subject matter, considering..." Her voice trails off, like she can't speak aloud what happened because then it will be true.

"Because my family is dead?"

Hanna chews on her lip and my words wipe the smile off Lyssa's face. "It's fine," I say, "That's why I'm thinking about ghosts." I lie down on Hanna's bed and the two of them follow suit, their heads resting against either side of mine.

"Do you think they're ghosts now?" Lyssa asks.

"I don't know," I say.

"I think they could be. You know, like if you asked them to be."

I'm not sure what that means, but I know Mom would have understood. She would have nodded thoughtfully and then pulled out a bag of crystals or something, and Dad would have eyed her over his book and smiled while shaking his head. Tansy would have asked to play with the crystals, and Rowan would have rushed through the room, late on his way to soccer practice, while Mom would have waved goodbye. And I would have been sitting there, watching it all, daydreaming about the day when I get to live on my own and explore the world.

That's what I always did—I was always just watching them and pretending to be somewhere else. And now I'm not sure who I'm supposed to watch anymore, and I'm not sure where I'm pretending to be.

"Do you think your dad's OK?" Lyssa asks. Hanna tenses up next to me—she's afraid of the answer.

"They'll find him," Hanna says, trying to be reassuring. She uses her Soft Hanna voice but her body gives her away because it's turned to steel beside me.

I nod even though I don't believe her. I didn't think my dad would leave me in that laurel bush, but he did, and so even though Hanna says they'll find him, I'm not so sure. I don't recognize my dad anymore; I don't recognize either of us. It's as if when the truck collided with Mom's car, it was us—Dad and me—that got scattered all over the road instead. Mom, Tansy, and Rowan all danced away into the air, leaving me and Dad in pieces.

Hanna and Lyssa wipe the tears from my eyes. Eventually, I fall asleep in Hanna's bed.

3

"Could you show me a recent picture of your father?"

Mrs. Jackson reaches in front of me and passes a photograph to the detective sitting across from us. It's as if I'm not even there—the question is directed toward me, but he only looks at Mrs. Jackson.

Mrs. Jackson pushes the picture across the table quickly, like she's afraid if I see it, I'll burst into tears. It isn't a completely ungrounded suspicion, seeing as I burst into tears this morning when she gave me breakfast because it reminded me of what it felt like to eat at a table with a family. Just a few weeks ago, we were eating meals together, and I wasn't paying much attention to them. Tansy was probably telling a story and Rowan was probably stuffing food into his face, and I was probably sitting there thinking about school or Hanna or something not related to my family whatsoever. And now, all I can think about is them, and their profound absence. They're not here. No one's here but me now.

I still manage to catch a glimpse of the picture, despite Mrs. Jackson's attempt to be discrete. It's a headshot they used at the university for my dad's professor profile. The lighting is pretty bad so his skin looks incredibly pale and his hair looks messy. He's smiling with his crooked teeth and his bow tie is crooked too. One time, Rowan and I checked his

Rate My Professors page and found that he had a chili pepper, which means some student out there thinks he's hot. We laughed about it for weeks. I'm still convinced it was Mom who went in there and rated him like that as an ego booster.

The detective tells us they still haven't found Dad, which is both good and bad, according to Mrs. Jackson. It's bad, of course, because he's not here. It's also good because they didn't find a body which means he's probably alive. That is, unless he's starved to death. Dad always liked to eat gourmet food, and frankly I can't imagine him surviving by catching and eating wildlife himself.

I shouldn't have to imagine him surviving on wildlife. *Dad, why did you leave?*

I close my eyes and picture Ghost Tansy holding my hand. She's scared, and she doesn't know where Dad is. Aren't ghosts supposed to know everything when they die? Then again, I'm making up Ghost Tansy in my head—she doesn't know where Dad is because I don't know either.

The past few weeks have required me to be at the police station for longer than I ever thought I would be in a lifetime. Mom and Dad called me the family rule follower, the peacekeeper. Dad said it was because I listened to Rowan get into trouble so much in our younger years that I decided to take the opposite approach. Mom said it was because my moon is in Virgo, though I'm still not entirely sure what that really means. I agreed with both of them because that was my role, but maybe I'm the way I am just because I was born like that—because I'm just Laurel Summers.

I'm even the peacekeeper among friends. Lyssa and Hanna sometimes argue because they have really different home lives and don't understand one another, and I'm always stuck in the middle. Except one time I fought with Lyssa for an entire summer—the year I decided I didn't want to be the rule follower anymore and I tried way too hard to become the "funny friend," a role that's always been reserved for Lyssa, our comic relief. At the end-of-year middle school awards Lyssa got voted "Most Likely to Become a Comedian" and I was so jealous about it I didn't talk to her all summer. I've given up on trying to be the funny one since then. We laugh about it now because we were only twelve and it felt like such a big deal at the time.

Mom would have never believed a rule follower like me could end up in a police station multiple times in one week. After we found her car that day, they took us to the nearest hospital and then to the morgue to identify the bodies, which was just as traumatizing as you can imagine.

Dad didn't want me to come with him. He said, "Really, Laurel, that's not necessary, they only need one person to identify the bodies." But I insisted and he agreed because he was too sad and lost to put up a fight.

Tansy was missing an arm. Rowan's face looked so cold and empty. I didn't look at Mom because they told us her face had been mutilated and we might not recognize her but because of procedure we still had to identify her. I closed my eyes because I didn't want to see Mom not looking like Mom. Dad kept his eyes open the whole time while crying a steady stream of tears.

After that they took us to the police station, where they talked to us about the man driving the car and how there would be a trial and he would likely be charged with three counts of manslaughter. That made me feel kind of sick, because it wasn't the driver who killed them, it was the car. I mean, it was him by association, as he was driving said car, but I don't even know what his face looks like and it's hard to place blame on somebody you've never met. Or maybe it's easier, and that's why I don't want to, because then it's like slipping into a cop-out. Instead of blaming the terribleness of the world, I could place all my blame on one man who made a left turn on a red light.

So this is the second time I've been to the police station and I really, really hope it's my last. The way the officers walk quickly past me and around the corners reminds me of that night. The night when Dad and I got here and they were telling us to follow them into a private room, asking us questions about what happened. Everything went so fast. Their blurred shapes moved fast and then everything moved fast around me. The memory sends a shiver down my spine.

"Take care," the police officer says as we stand to leave. His words make my teeth clench. I don't know how I'm supposed to "take care" without my parents or my siblings. Who am I taking care of exactly? Who's taking care of me?

Mrs. Jackson puts her arm around me and walks me out of the police station to meet Hanna, who's waiting for us outside. Mrs. Jackson says something reassuring, along the lines of "They'll find him soon, Laurel," and I nod and give her a quick smile. She seems worried and my natural peacekeeping instincts command that I try and make others feel like it'll be OK too.

The sun shines brightly in my face and it feels like the world is taunting me with its happiness. It's the beginning of summer, yet my world is falling apart. I'm supposed to be spending my days at the lake and staying up late watching movies.

Hanna says, "Let's go," and links her arm through mine—guiding me to the car. I keep my head down because I'm afraid if I look up, I'll see somebody from school, or somebody who knew my mom, and they'll give me *that* look: the pity look. The one that says, *I read about your family dying on the internet, and I'm going to say I'm sorry because I don't know what else to say.*

I'm so, so glad it's summer. Since it's summer, this will fizzle out by the time school starts. Which, in part, is an absolutely horrifying truth—*how does something like having a dead family fizzle out?* But at least I won't have to be at school while the news circulates. The news has already circulated—I've noticed from the excessive number of social media posts and texts. Mom always said I was addicted to social media, but she'd be pleased to know I can't stand being on it for more than a second since she died. Maybe her lasting wish was for me to log out of Instagram. Wish granted, Mom.

I don't even want to go back to familiar places. Like school. Maybe I won't. This counts as an extenuating circumstance, and since Dad is gone, maybe I'll be sent to live with my grandparents in Arizona and will never have to set foot in my high school again. Part of me welcomes a change that would wipe the slate clean, but I also feel conflicted about leaving Hanna and Lyssa. The three of us are in this together. That's how it's always been.

I can't remember the exact last thing I said to my family—probably something mundane about pizza. Isn't that what you're supposed to remember when people die? Like somehow the last words I say to them are supposed to stick, glued into my mind forever, and I'm supposed to tattoo those words onto my body to honor them. But I don't remember what we said to one another. I couldn't tell you if my life depended on it. It was probably about pizza.

"You can take me home," I say. Hanna and Mrs. Jackson glance at one another and Hanna bites her lip.

"I don't think that's a good idea," Mrs. Jackson says.

"But what if my dad is at home?" I know that it's just a pipe dream the minute it slips out of my mouth. The words taste sour and my face turns red and my eyes water.

"We could just swing by," Hanna suggests. "Laurel can grab some clothes and see if he's there. We can walk home from there, Mom. Then you can be alone and get work done."

"Pumpkin," I add. "I need to feed Pumpkin." Pumpkin is the family Jack Russell terrier, and I feel like an absolutely terrible person for forgetting about him, yet I'm also mad. What was Dad planning to do? Just leave our dog to starve? The thought makes me sick, and the worry in my stomach turns to low-simmering anger.

"Well…OK," Mrs. Jackson agrees. Mrs. Jackson works from home. She's an interior designer and is always busy planning out things for new clients or having important phone calls.

My house looks the same (I was only just there yesterday)—tan-painted walls and a dark blue door, two stories, bright and homey. Anyone walking by would have no clue that half the members of the house are now dead and have been dead for nearly two weeks. The garden is still impeccable because the flowers haven't started to droop yet. It'll be a matter of days before they do. Mom was the gardener. She used to spend all her time in our yard, and now it looks so lonely without her presence.

The inside of the house is like the outside—it doesn't feel any different. It doesn't feel haunted or empty or broken. It feels the same with the exception of light dust on the stair posts because nobody's been dusting. The sameness is a choking, suffocating thing because everything is as far from "the same" as possible. This time, when I return, I still have cuts on my face from the laurel bush, and my skin crawls with ghosts and my legs are weak, like jelly.

Pumpkin greets me with so much enthusiasm it feels wrong. I don't know how he could be so happy. There's nothing to be happy about anymore. He licks my face and hops on my feet and I wonder if he's realized they're gone forever yet. This isn't just a family vacation—this is forever. His ignorance, a dog's oblivious state of optimism, makes me really sad. I put food in his bowl and I run my fingers through his short hair. Hanna slips out of our way and lingers near the door. She watches me anxiously as I walk farther into the house.

Dad's not home. I know he's not. There are no car keys on the counter and his phone isn't plugged into the wall and he hasn't left his shoes sitting out on the doormat. In my ear Ghost Tansy whispers for me to pack Benny, her stuffed rabbit. Ghost Rowan tells me I should grab my volleyball bag because I really should be practicing since I'm headed into sophomore year and I need to make varsity, or at least junior varsity. Beside me, Pumpkin barks. I wonder if he hears them too.

"Dad?" I call out. Pumpkin follows at my heels as I make my way through the otherwise empty house. Ghost Tansy pulls on me, trying to drag me up the stairs and to her room. "Dad?" I call again. This time, it's my own voice that sounds underwater.

It's the note on my bed that does it. One word messily scrawled with one of Dad's favorite ballpoint pens. "Sorry."

He knew. He knew he wasn't going to come back—he'd been planning it all along. What was he thinking? That he'd just bring me along for the ride? That he'd leave Pumpkin behind to feed himself? I hold the slip of paper in my hands, shaking slightly, and the softness inside of me disappears. I emerge from the underwater prison and my lungs are on fire. I feel dangerous and combustible, like if I don't do something soon I'm going to explode and take the world down with me.

Still gripping the note, I walk as if in a trance into Dad and Mom's room—just Dad's room, now. Photographs of smiling moments line the walls; Tansy's old elementary-school drawings are framed. The bedsheets are messy and unmade, even though Dad has been sleeping downstairs ever since the accident.

Before I can stop myself, I'm lifting one of the photographs from the wall. It's heavy in my hands, which shake as I stare at our smiling faces. It's a picture from last spring—I remember taking it, because Dad made a big deal of using the timer camera on his phone, and it took nearly ten tries to get it right. We're outdoors in the backyard with Mom's garden in full-color display behind us. Pumpkin's even in it, in Mom's arms, with his tongue hanging out the side of his mouth.

And then, I smash it. I grab another frame from the wall, too, and let the glass crack against the wall. They shatter into tons of tiny shards and scrape the images, blurring the happy family out of existence. If Dad was here, he would stop me, but he's not here. I tear his coats off the hangers and toss them across the floor, wrenching them so hard that the bar creaks and falls out of place, sending clothes cascading onto the floor. Why isn't he here?

Pumpkin barks at me, backs away, and watches from a safe distance. I kick at the bedpost. Hanna's footsteps grow nearer as she ascends the stairs. I move toward Dad's dresser and push all the cologne off the top of it. The bottles smash onto the floor and the room smells so strongly that my eyes start to sting. I'm about to knock the gadgets from his bedside table—he likes to keep them on display so neatly—but Hanna gets here before I can. She grabs my arms mid-swing and holds them behind my back.

"I'm going to kill him," I say, hot tears rolling down my cheeks. "I'm going to kill him for disappearing. He did it on purpose! He did it on purpose, Hanna!"

Hanna wraps her arms around me and holds tight to keep me from swinging again. She's smaller than me, yet I give in and crumple against her.

"You're not going to kill him," she says softly. "You're going to find him."

But what kind of daughter is supposed to be held responsible for finding her dad? Not me; it shouldn't be me. That was Rowan's job as the oldest—he always took care of our parents even though he complained about it. Or Tansy, the one with all the big ideas. If Tansy was here, she'd probably know where Dad is by now. She'd treat it like a big mystery game. I'm the one who's supposed to keep the peace. But who needs peace if they're all gone? Who do I bring peace to now?

Eventually, Hanna stops restraining me and our bodies soften into a hug. She runs her hands up and down my arms, which reminds me I'm alive and not just a fuming pile of a person left on the road beside my mom's broken car. I'm not shattered there. I'm whole here. I'm the only Summers kid left, even if I'm not much of a person anymore.

"I'll get you some clothes," Hanna mumbles, finally releasing me. "Do you care what I pick?"

I shake my head and she turns to walk toward my room, carefully looking back at me to make sure I'm not about to explode again. Pumpkin curls up on my feet. He likes to sit on feet—it's one of his many quirks. Hanna emerges from my room with a duffel bag full of clothes. We haven't been alone since the kiss—the weirdness still clings to the air around us, and now we're alone in my house just outside the room where it happened. Most of the weirdness has moved aside, replaced by grief, which takes up a lot of space in a relationship, whether it's a friendship or something else.

Before we leave, I grab Benny the stuffed rabbit and my volleyball bag. Hanna takes Pumpkin's leash and says, "I already texted my mom. It's fine if Pumpkin comes with us." Relief washes over me. I could not leave him alone another night. He's all I've got left—it's just me and the family dog with no family left. Pumpkin jumps up and down when he sees the leash, and I feel better because it means I'll get to sleep in bed with him tonight.

I linger by the door for a moment, hoping Dad will pop up out of the blue and have a perfectly good explanation for his absence. If he popped up out of the blue right now—I might not even need a good explanation. I might just run into his arms and take back everything I just screamed about in the house and offer to replace everything I broke. Except he doesn't pop up, and instead Hanna takes my hand and we walk to her house in silence.

4

Perhaps I've completely lost my mind, but Ghost Mom showed up last night. Maybe she was upset with me for breaking all of Dad's things, although she didn't say anything about it. She just held me and told me it's OK to feel all the things I feel, which made me cry so hard I got up and hid in Hanna's bathroom so I wouldn't wake her or the whole household. "I'm so sorry," Ghost Mom told me. I don't know exactly what she was apologizing for because none of this is her fault, but somehow it made me feel better and worse at the same time. I sobbed harder but a warmth spread inside me because her ghost arms were around me, holding me in that bathroom.

I don't exactly have a track record of seeing ghosts or believing in witchy things—in fact, I have a stronger track record of watching too much reality TV and always turning down homecoming dates. But now I'm seeing ghosts. Or rather, feeling them.

Apparently, that's just what happens when people you love die. I've got to hold on to them somehow, and if Ghost Mom follows me around forever, I won't complain. She's warm, not cold like ghosts are in the books. She's much warmer than Ghost Rowan (who's rather cold) and Ghost Tansy (who's a lukewarm temperature). She makes me feel lighter, like she's holding some of my bags while I walk along. She tucked me into bed right next to Pumpkin, once I finally stopped crying, and I slept so deeply I actually felt refreshed when I woke up. So, I guess I'm fine with Ghost Mom hanging around. As long as Ghost Dad doesn't show up, because he's supposed to be alive. He's supposed to be with me right now, instead of leaving me alone at Hanna's house.

I have a feeling this summer is going to be lonelier than every other summer that's come before it. I've been constantly surrounded by people since everyone heard about the accident, but I'm still painfully lonely. That's one of those things about summer—the season is incredibly lonesome. The freedom of summer is always romanticized, but the reality is summer is mostly spent sitting at home, flipping through channels on the television, and doing dumb chores for your parents. Waiting for your friends to text you back only to find that your schedules don't match up because you all have summer jobs or family vacations and plans fall through the cracks, despite the illusion of summer freedom. And for me, the loneliness of summer is now amplified by my dead family and my missing dad.

"Good morning." Mrs. Jackson smiles at me. She has a dress on because it's a Sunday, which means she's forcing Hanna to attend Mass with her and will then spend the rest of the day raving about how good the sermon was. "Toast?" she asks and pushes a plate in front of me with a piece covered in strawberry-red jam.

"Thanks, Mrs. Jackson."

"Hanna's outside." Hanna is always up before me. At sleepovers, Hanna would be first, then me, and then Lyssa. Lyssa could sleep through a stampede of elephants, and Hanna would wake up to the sound of a feather falling to the floor.

I glance out the window. Hanna and her dad are sitting on a bench swing drinking their tea. Hanna and her dad resemble one another physically the same way Hanna and her mom resemble one another with their mannerisms. It's a picture-perfect image of family and it makes my heart break into a million bits. Mrs. Jackson doesn't notice my heart scattered all around the room; she just tells me I need to eat.

"We're going to service today," she tells me as she removes my plate after I've sufficiently picked at the toast. "You're welcome to join us."

Mrs. Jackson has been trying to get Dad and me to go to church with her since the accident. We had the funeral in a church, mostly for Grandma's sake, and I don't think either of us wants to set foot in another church any time soon. Mom was Buddhist anyways and Dad denounced religion when he was seven years old, much to Grandma's disappointment.

"I think I'll stay here," I say.

"Church can be very healing in times like these."

I would have choked on my toast if I was still chewing on it. My throat constricts around her words anyway. *Times like these.* What's that supposed to mean? Is losing the majority of your family in a car accident a common thing that happens to people? She's talking about it like it's some sort of rite of passage.

"I'd rather not today," I say. "Yesterday was kind of a bad day for me, and I don't really want to go out into public. And besides, I can stay here and make sure Pumpkin doesn't destroy the place." Pumpkin is the least destructive dog I've ever met. Mrs. Jackson knows that, but she nods and pats me on the shoulder because she knows I'm not going to budge.

"I'll have John stay here with you."

"You don't have to."

"Lyssa could come over. Or you could go there?"

She knows that me going to Lyssa's house is a moot point because Lyssa is at a foster home and she doesn't like inviting people over to stay with her foster parents. But Mrs. Jackson has made it apparent that she doesn't want me to be left alone. What does she think I'm going to do? Off myself? I mean, I guess I don't blame her for being afraid of that. My mom, sister, and brother died and my dad abandoned me. God. It sounds like something out of a drama show with the most unrealistic, tragic circumstances ever.

"Sure," I say. "I'll invite Lyssa over."

"Good." Mrs. Jackson smiles.

"She's totally judging you for not going to church," says Ghost Rowan's voice in my ear.

"Shut up," I mutter.

"What was that?" Mrs. Jackson gives me a weird look.

"Nothing."

She keeps looking at me weird and then turns back to washing the dishes. *Great,* I think, *now I'm talking to ghosts out loud.*

Hanna and her parents leave for church. Hanna is wearing a dress even though she hates dresses, and I make a point to tell her she looks nice even though she only grimaces in response. Hanna is one of those people who has pink folders and binders and likes to be girly but still hates wearing dresses. I like that about her; she doesn't fit into a box. Not that anybody really fits into a box.

It's lonely in the Jackson house after they leave, lonelier than ever before. The loneliness hits like a wave; there's nobody here to tell me to do dishes or give me allowance or force me to go to school on days when I'd much rather sleep in. For a moment, I consider leaving—packing a bag, putting Pumpkin's leash on, walking out and seeing where we end up. I could live on the road, change my name, possibly become a psychic or a medium, since I've acquired a new mystical ability to talk to my dead family. Either that, or I've lost my mind. How does a person become a psychic or a medium, anyways? Do I send in a resume that says I talk to my dead mom and siblings and then they hand me a job? It's worth a shot.

I would cut off all my hair and completely shave my head clean. Perhaps then it would grow back vibrant red, like Mom's, and I'd look like a proper Summers child.

Except I don't run away, because how often do people actually run away? Everyone thinks about running away but nobody ever actually does it, unless they're exceptionally brave or exceptionally unlucky. Technically, I fall into that exceptionally unlucky category, but I still don't run away because—well, I don't know—that's just the way I am. I'm not adventurous or brave or spirited. I'm just Laurel. I'm consistent. Predictable. And, according to Lyssa, occasionally "bland."

Maybe, at one point, I had dreams of running away, but they were premeditated and safe—I would go to college overseas or travel the world for a summer. Now, I'm not even sure what I'm going to do tomorrow. Everything has toppled over.

As if on cue, Lyssa shows up to squash all my remaining urges to run. "Heya," she says, waltzing in through Hanna's garage door like everything is normal. Pumpkin kisses her on the face and she scratches him behind the ears. That's what I love most about Lyssa—she always behaves like everything is normal even though it's not. It's calming, especially now.

"Cut my hair," I say, or more like demand.

"You serious? I have clippers in my purse." Of course she does.

"Yes. Shave it all off."

"You're weird."

Rowan used to always tell me I wasn't weird enough. He said I needed more of a personality. "Your looks are just average. If you're going to date any guys, you're going to need to be quirky." I hated it when he made that comment—I even hated *him* when he made that comment. "Like me," he said.

"Our family isn't the most attractive bunch, but I'm good at soccer and I have a great personality. That's why girls like me."

I punched him in the arm when he said that. Then Tansy asked, "What does getting laid mean?" and Rowan and I both burst out laughing. Tansy got mad and stomped away. That's the way it always was with Rowan and me—we would fight but then we would laugh, and I wouldn't think too much about the things he said because he was my brother and brothers say stupid things. Hanna says they shouldn't be allowed to say stupid things.

She says boys can get away with whatever they want and that isn't fair. She's not wrong. A part of me resents Rowan for that, and sometimes I wonder if Mom resented Rowan for that too. Mom would always shake her head and say, "I didn't raise you to say those things."

Lyssa is about to shave my entire head of hair off when my phone rings.

"Let it go," I say.

"It's a local number."

"It's probably not important."

Lyssa answers for me anyways. She drops the clippers and they nearly slice her toes off, I swear.

Dad. They found my dad.

Within an hour of receiving that call, I'm fast-walking down the hospital corridors to find Dad. When I step into the room directly behind the nurses that guide me to him, and I look him in the eyes, I don't recognize him. This is not Dad.

Well technically, it is Dad. He says, "I'm sorry, Laurel," with so much brokenness it sounds as if the entire world has fallen apart. That's not Dad—that's a shell of the person he was, the person he could have been. Dads aren't supposed to sound like that—it should be illegal.

It turns out some park rangers found him wandering off the trail near the hiking path he'd taken us on. He was starving and thirsty and they had to restrain him to bring him to the hospital. He kept saying he hadn't found what he was looking for. Now he's in a psych ward. I guess he wasn't looking for that.

My very own father—who was always the calm one in the family—in a psych ward. Mom would have never suspected it, and she spent a few years working as a therapist when I was pretty young. She quit because it was too much for her. Afterward, she would always say that our family was blessed with a clean slate—no history of mental illness. And yet somehow, my dad is in a psych ward.

I don't get much time with Dad because within minutes, he's dozed off due to the high doses of sedatives he's taking.

As he drifts away, his eyes slowly closing and his face relaxing, I catch a glimpse of the way things used to be before the accident. He sleeps peacefully, and it almost makes all of this so much worse.

Behind me, Hanna says, "Stop thinking so much." She stands in the doorway, her shadow falling over me. My guess is that Lyssa called her the moment we got here, or the police called Mrs. Jackson to let her know.

"I'm not thinking."

"You're always thinking."

"No. It's actually possible to stand somewhere and not think, not that you would know." Hanna is the one who is always thinking—her brain is always moving full speed ahead.

"Don't be a smartass."

"Don't swear."

She grins at me. Once when we were in middle school, Hanna didn't talk to me for a full week because she said I swore too much. I learned all the best curse words from Rowan. He always had a foul mouth, as Mom would say. *Would have said.* Now, whenever Hanna swears, I tell her not to as an ode to our stupid week-long fight over my choice of words. Hanna doesn't care about swearing anymore, except for the word "bitch." She hates that one because she says it's too derogatory. Unfortunately for her, it's also Lyssa's favorite swear word.

I *am* thinking, but if Hanna could see what's going on inside of my head, she'd probably run away screaming. At school I smile a lot and I play sports and I once ran for class secretary in the eighth grade and won. I'm normal—painfully normal— except in my head it feels like everything is all jumbled up and the past few weeks I've felt things slipping through the cracks. And now, I'm severely not normal because I'm the girl with the dead family and the psych-ward dad.

I hate that, I really do. I hate being that stereotype of the girl who's laughing on the outside and dying on the inside.

That's not who I am. I'm sometimes laughing on the outside but I'm not dying on the inside—I'm just jumbled. Isn't everyone? And now I'm not so sure what I am. I'm jumbled on the outside and the inside. My whole world is jumbled and now I'm the only one left to put the pieces back together.

"You should go home," Hanna whispers.

She has a point. It's still light outside, the sun barely beginning to dip in the sky, and my whole body already radiates with the exhaustion of the day.

"I want to be here if he wakes up."

"I know you do. But you need to sleep too."

"I will."

She sighs and turns to leave. I listen to her footsteps disappear down the hallway. It's just me and Dad in the hospital room now and I want him to wake up again so badly, even if he's still in a sedated state. I want him to wake up so I can ask him what he was looking for on that mountain. What was so important? What was more important than me lying in the laurel bush? I should have asked him first thing, instead of nodding at his apology and letting the nurses brush past me to give him medication. I should have screamed at him and demanded an answer, an explanation. But I didn't, because I'm me. All I ever do is stand aside while things happen all around me.

"What were you looking for?" I whisper, standing close to his bed. He doesn't hear me because he's asleep. His body looks weak and frail, even though he was only out there for slightly more than two days. I don't know if he's eaten much since Mom and Rowan and Tansy died—I haven't been paying enough attention. Maybe I'm the one who abandoned him; maybe I left myself behind in the laurel bush.

"Visiting hours are almost up." A nurse with a nice smile stands in the doorway, where Hanna was just minutes ago.

"He's my dad."

"Your mom is waiting out there for you." My heart flutters for a minute because the thought of Mom waiting for me makes me feel warm inside. I miss her, and then I remember why I miss her.

"That's not my mom."

"Is it an aunt?"

"It's my friend's mom."

"Oh. OK. She's waiting for you. Why don't you go home and get some rest?"

"My mom is dead," I say. I don't know why I say it—I'm letting all the jumbled things in my head slip out through my mouth. It's like I've forgotten what parts of me go on the inside and what parts go on the outside.

The nurse swallows and scratches his head. "I'm sorry."

"Why do people always say that?"

"I don't—"

"Too many people have been saying that to me. I don't want to hear it anymore. Really. Don't say it again."

He frowns and I'm afraid he's about to apologize again, but then he bites his lip and stops himself. "We have a social worker on staff if you need to talk to somebody."

Talking to somebody sounds nice, but I'd much rather talk to this nurse, because he's here right now and the social worker feels like a cop-out for him. Plus the social worker might be sad like Mom was when she was a therapist, and I don't want to add to their sadness.

"I'm going to sleep in the waiting room." I don't think he cares. He just nods and tells me to let him know if I need anything. I give Dad's weak, sleeping body one last glance before leaving the room.

Hanna, Lyssa, and Mrs. Jackson are out in the waiting room. Mrs. Jackson sits with her laptop balancing on her knees, hunched over and frowning at the screen. Hanna is pacing while Lyssa scrolls through something on her phone.

They all look up when I enter the hall. Mrs. Jackson stands and embraces me while Hanna closes her laptop for her and slides it into her bag.

I want to stay because I can't leave Dad, so I tell them that. Mrs. Jackson frowns and bites her lip, a nervous tic just like Hanna's. "Laurel, you really need some rest in a proper bed."

"I don't want to leave him."

"We can come back tomorrow morning. He's sleeping now, anyway."

"I have to ask him questions."

"You can do that tomorrow—"

"No."

"I'll stay with you," Lyssa chimes in. She puts an arm around me and smiles. "Hospital sleepover!"

"Won't your foster family be mad?"

She shrugs. "They're cool. They know all about you. They can't really say no to my newly orphaned best friend."

Hanna sucks in a breath, attempting to stifle a gasp, and I laugh.

"Not entirely orphaned, sorry," Lyssa continues, grinning at me and ignoring Hanna. "Your dad's just…out of commission."

"That's one way to put it."

"Hanna?" Mrs. Jackson interrupts, raising her eyebrows at her daughter and standing impatiently.

"I'll come home." She grimaces. "I've got my class tomorrow." She squeezes my shoulder and adds, "I'll feed Pumpkin for you. My dad's been watching him all day, even took him to the park. Wouldn't be surprised if my dad suggested we get a dog of our own soon."

Hanna may be one of the only people I know who actively signs up for summer classes. Not the kind that are mandatory for kids who don't pass their classes; rather, the kind that the super smart kids take to, as Hanna would put it, "get ahead." She's taking some advanced math summer course full of equally nerdy teenagers, so it's basically camp but for math geeks.

Hanna's always trying to prove something to someone. I haven't quite figured out what or who yet; maybe it's her mom. I think about the night we kissed and she started crying and begged me not to tell anyone—maybe she was afraid of what her mom would think. Hanna's always working hard on some project she's assigned herself or some extracurricular she signed up for. For instance, last year, she created this whole campaign to try and get the school cafeteria to provide more vegan options. It didn't go anywhere, but she still says it'll pick up. I wonder if she hopes that maybe, if she exceeds in everything she possibly can, her mom won't care that she kissed a girl. I would hope that by now, people have stopped caring so much about that, but Mrs. Jackson is really involved in her church.

After Hanna and her mom finally leave, Lyssa and I sit next to one another in the uncomfortable chairs of the hospital waiting room. The other people here look like they'll be spending the night too: a boy who is probably our age, a mom and her toddler-aged daughter, an old man who's holding a necklace in his hands and rubbing it between his fingers.

"It's like *The Breakfast Club*, but sadder," Lyssa whispers. A bunch of unlikely people stuck in a room, forced to spend time together. Except it's not a movie so we don't all bond and share sob stories—instead we drift in and out of sleep in uncomfortable waiting-room chairs.

"Sorry I never cut off all your hair," Lyssa whispers.

"Next time I get a hair-cutting impulse, I'll call you."

"Glad I'm your go-to."

She leans her head on my shoulder.

"Laurel?" she whispers.

"Mmm?"

"Are you in love with Hanna?"

I don't say anything back. She snuggles into me.

"I'm not blind," she continues.

"You are when you're not wearing contacts."

We both giggle and I feel the tension leave my chest, at least for a few breaths, until I remember that I shouldn't feel relieved right now. My family is dead—I'm supposed to be the heaviest person on earth carrying all these bags of grief. Right?

But Dad is alive and Lyssa knows I'm in love with Hanna and she doesn't care that we're both girls and we're also both her best friends. Everything could blow up in our faces and she'd be left to pick up all the pieces. I feel light even though I'm supposed to feel heavy right now.

"Good night," Lyssa mumbles.

"Good night."

In the morning, Lyssa is gone. She's left a note beside my chair to tell me that she went to work, and there's also a blanket on top of me. I wonder if Lyssa put it there or if it was a nurse. Maybe it was the nurse who said he was sorry for my loss—he must have felt sorry about saying sorry.

I tiptoe into Dad's room only to find him sitting there wide awake. The ghost of a smile haunts his face. The corners of his mouth twitch, like he's trying really hard to look happy. Then it disappears and he's crying big, fat tears. I want to look away. I'm not supposed to see my dad like this, but I can't peel my eyes off of him. Tears are flowing down my face too. I hold his hand and tell him it's OK, because that's what Mom would have done, though I really don't believe the words I say.

Lyssa says I'm the only teenager in the world who doesn't absolutely hate crying. I used to cry a lot as a kid. I was that one girl who would cry when somebody spelled her name wrong. Honestly, when I think back on it, it's a little embarrassing how emotional I was in elementary school. One time, my second-grade teacher asked for a meeting with my parents to talk about my emotional regulation. Mom got really mad and told my teacher she was trying to censor my feelings. Mom always said crying was like poetry. I still don't really understand what she meant. She made crying seem like a beautiful thing, so it doesn't hurt me as much as it hurts other people. It just feels natural, like eating or drinking or falling asleep. And for the record, eventually I stopped crying in class all the time.

Dad's eyes are closed as the tears pour down his cheeks. He looks so broken I can't bring myself to ask him what he was looking for on the trail. I want to, but I don't. I'm not ready to know what he thought was more important than me. What if it was something insignificant? Not that I'm the most important thing in the world, but Dad is all I have left. That has to mean something.

The doctors say they're going to keep him at least another night to make sure he's stable. According to them, he was suicidal and manic—two words I never thought I would hear in reference to my dad. Then again, I also never thought my mom and siblings would die because a truck driver didn't pay attention to the color of a traffic light. My world is inverted.

"Quinton! Laurel!" The door to Dad's hospital room swings open and in walk his parents, Grandma Lucy and Grandpa Rubin. They must have flown in, which is a surprise to me—I bet they've been trying to contact me. I haven't had my phone on. Grandma Lucy is out of breath. She's wearing a bright red shawl, the same shade as her cheeks. It's wrapped around her shoulders and looks like it's about to fall off and slide to the floor. Grandpa Rubin appears confused, with an ever-present frown on his face. His jacket is slightly wrinkled.

"I should have stayed after the funeral," Grandma Lucy says as she rushes over to Dad's bedside. They were here a few weeks ago for the funeral but then they went back home. Grandma runs her own business painting houses and she had clients and Dad told her he would be OK, that they could fly back when she had more time in her schedule. And now, they're back. They flew in this morning, they tell me.

"Nobody called me to tell me he disappeared!" Grandma exclaims. I guess in the mess of it all I didn't think to call them. "And now he's in the hospital? I knew we should have stayed, Rubin. Laurel, all by herself!"

Laurel, all by herself. That's my life now.

Grandma says I need to go home and sleep in a proper bed.

"I don't want to," I say. "I need to stay here, with Dad. Right, Dad?"

Dad doesn't say anything. He just cries and then takes the pills the nurse hands him, and within minutes, he's drifted off again. He looks peaceful when he sleeps, more peaceful than he's ever looked before, even when Mom was alive.

"Really, now, let's get you home. We're staying at your place until all this settles down." I don't know if it'll ever settle down. I want to yell at Grandma but I bite my tongue and say, "I want to stay," and she shakes her head. Grandpa doesn't talk—he's never been much of a talker. He gave all his talking to Grandma.

Maybe they should have stayed after the funeral. It's all kind of blurry to me. That's how sadness works—it smudges memories like water spilled over inky paper. I remember Grandma and Grandpa sitting downstairs with Dad in the living room the night after the funeral. Grandma sounded very worried but Dad told her to go home and said we'd be OK. I remember standing there on the stairs in my pajamas wondering if we really would be OK. Grandma and Grandpa left and things got blurry again and then Dad and I were in the car driving to the trail and then Dad disappeared.

"Laurel, we need you to go home. Please, honey."

I'm saved, once again, by Hanna and Lyssa. They walk into the waiting room just as Grandma tries to drag me out the door.

"Oh!" Hanna says when she sees my grandparents. She smiles wide and says, "Hi!" They've known Hanna for a few years now, and they've always loved her—especially Grandpa. He loves how organized she is because he's a lot like that too. One time, he spent nearly an hour showing her how he organizes his binders full of biographies of my family members going all the way back to the 1890s.

"Hi, Hanna, dear. And Alyssa, right?"

"Just Lyssa."

"Lyssa."

Lyssa's full name is Alyssa, but she likes being called Lyssa because she thinks it's more unique. She decided to be Lyssa when she went into foster care. I didn't know her very well before she was in foster care, so she's always been Lyssa to me.

"We were just trying to get Laurel to go home." Grandma doesn't release her grip on my arm; she's trying to keep me in place. Doesn't she understand I want to stay close to Dad? Even though it feels like I don't know him anymore, I still want to stay close to him. I can't let him disappear again.

Hanna nods. "That's a good idea, Laurel. You really do need to go home. Your dad will be fine here."

I shoot her a look and she rolls her eyes. "You need sleep."

"She slept last night," Lyssa says. "I stayed with her. Waiting-room chairs are oddly not as uncomfortable as you'd expect."

"Come on," Grandma says, ignoring Lyssa's comments. "Your dad is asleep. We can come back after you get some rest and some proper food. He'll be awake by then."

"I—"

"Oh, let her stay." Grandpa speaks for the first time since his arrival. "We can go to the house, do some cleaning and cooking, feed the dog, and then come back."

"I fed him this morning," Hanna says. "He's been staying with us. But I'm sure he'd love a nice walk, if you want me to drop him off!"

"That would be wonderful, Hanna."

Grandma can't argue with Grandpa. He never strikes up arguments with her—she's a force to be reckoned with—so when he does, she knows he has good reason. She makes a "harrumph" sound and then squeezes my hand. "We'll be back in a few hours, OK Laurel?"

"OK."

She looks tired. I see it in her eyes. Obviously, everything has been absolutely terrible for Dad and me, but it must be a different kind of terrible for her too because she has to be a parent to Dad and a grandparent to me. Or even a parent to me too, because I am somewhat parentless at the moment. Dad practically exists in another universe right now, despite physically sitting in a hospital bed only a few feet away from me, and Mom, well…Mom's gone.

"We'll stay here with her," Hanna reassures them, even though just moments ago she was agreeing with Grandma about taking me home. That's how Hanna is: she thinks she knows what's best for other people, but if I tell her it's not what's best for me, she listens. For a stubborn person, she changes her mind easily. As for me, I'm like Grandpa—I don't pick up arguments unless I have a good reason to, and Hanna knows that. Hanna will argue about anything, but when I disagree, it's a rarity.

People are all just recycled versions of other people. I'm like Grandpa and also Mom and Dad and even Rowan and Tansy. And Hanna is like her mom, and sometimes she reminds me of my grandma, but I don't know where that came from. And Lyssa always dyes her hair to match whatever celebrity or character she's obsessed with. It's like how books are all just recycled letters and words strung together in different ways to make different stories. That's how people are: we're all recycled stories.

"Laurel?" Hanna asks. "Are you going to sleep here again tonight?"

I shrug.

"We'll stay with you," Lyssa says.

Hanna nods in agreement. "I even brought an emergency sleeping bag. It's in my car."

I laugh because that's a very Hanna thing to do. She's always prepared for most situations. But sometimes I wonder if she'd be happier if she did things she wasn't prepared for, like when she kissed me.

I shouldn't be thinking about that with everything that's going on, but I am. I can feel Ghost Mom smiling at me, asking me to tell her how it happened. *It was late, and we were watching a movie, and then it just sort of happened. It wasn't anything dramatic, and afterward, Hanna started to cry.*

If I had gotten to tell Mom, she would have sighed as if it was the greatest first-kiss story on the planet. Mom was always a very sappy person; she had a love for cheesy romance movies and romance novels with predictable plotlines. Deep down, Dad is very sappy too. He had to have been at one point to fall for someone like Mom. Maybe that's why he wound up in the hospital—when she died, all her sappiness latched onto him and it was just too much for one person to bear.

Eventually, Dad wakes up in time for dinner. Hanna and Lyssa join me in his room and we eat hospital cafeteria food while Lyssa tells him a story about her foster family's dog. Dad smiles when she talks about the time the dog jumped up on the counter and stole an entire piece of steak. Even though Lyssa is laughing and Dad and Hanna are smiling, the thickness of the situation chokes the air around us. Dad is in a psych ward, my family is dead, everything is very different. It feels wrong to have such a familiar, casual conversation.

"How come we haven't met your foster parents yet?" Dad asks Lyssa.

She shrugs. "I'll probably move around soon."

"Do you know that for sure?"

She shrugs again. Dad smiles at Lyssa like he knows something she doesn't. "I'd like to meet them. Wouldn't you, Laurel?"

I nod. Lyssa says, "Sometime soon, Mr. Summers," but I'm pretty sure she's just saying it for Dad's sake. I wonder how many nice things people have been saying to me lately just because they feel bad that my family is dead.

When we get up to leave the room, Ghost Tansy taps my shoulder, telling me to look at Dad. I turn around and meet his eyes, which are sad and teary, and once Lyssa and Hanna are out of earshot, he whispers something only I can hear. "I see them. I see them everywhere," he says.

"Me too," I tell him. When I breathe in, the pieces of Mom and Tansy and Rowan floating around in the air clog up my lungs. I see those pieces of them all around me, latching onto people who walk like Rowan, or dress like Mom, or smile like Tansy.

"I'm sorry," he says, his voice choking up again. I don't think he's talking about seeing ghosts anymore.

"Me too," I reply, because I don't think I've forgiven him for leaving. And then I walk out to the lobby and Hanna unrolls her sleeping bag in the middle of the room. The nurse who told me he was sorry yesterday comes in and hands us some extra blankets, and he doesn't say sorry this time. Instead he smiles, which is so much better than an apology.

Our sleeping companions are once again a hodgepodge of people. A twenty-year-old man, a sixteen-year-old girl and her younger sibling, and a middle-aged woman who keeps biting her nails. Grandma and Grandpa come back around midnight and settle into chairs near the three of us. I tell them they can go home because I know Grandpa has a bad back, but he shakes his head and says, "It's my son in the hospital room. Of course I'm staying here."

Grandpa starts snoring. Grandma leans on his shoulder and closes her eyes. As I start to drift off, Lyssa speaks.

"Are you still thinking about ghosts?" she asks quietly.

"Yeah," I whisper.

"Me too," she says.

I close my eyes and let sleep take me.

Less than a week passes before Dad finally gets to go home. He's under strict orders to take antidepressants and see a therapist, but he's stable and isn't as weak and scrawny looking as he was when they found him in the woods. They recommend that I look into therapy too, though I'm fairly certain that Dad should be the priority here. I'm not the one who went missing for days in the woods looking for who knows what.

"You really should think about going," Hanna says matter-of-factly.

"Maybe," I say, although she knows I won't. She shakes her head and I know she thinks I should go to therapy, but she also knows I'm not going to change my mind until I want to.

Mrs. Jackson drives Dad and me home from the hospital. For the whole ride, he stares out the window and doesn't speak to any of us, other than saying a quick thank-you to Mrs. Jackson for driving. It's like if he says something, he's going to start crying again, and he doesn't want to do that in front of me anymore. I don't blame him—I don't want him to do that in front of me anymore either, which feels like a terrible, selfish thing to admit.

Grandma and Grandpa made a cake at home that says "WELCOME HOME QUINTON" in large, slightly sloppy capital letters. Dad shakes his head because it's exactly the sort of thing my grandparents would do. If only they had made a banner too. But what would it say? "Congrats! You didn't kill yourself!" I shiver at the thought, which makes Grandma give me a look, but I keep my mouth shut.

Pumpkin is the most excited to see Dad. He jumps all over him and Dad starts crying when Pumpkin licks his face, which makes Pumpkin lick more, because his tears are salty, and Dad makes a noise that's somewhere between a laugh and a cry. Pumpkin is a very good dog. I wonder if he knows now. I wonder if he can smell the grief on us—if he's figured out that Mom and Tansy and Rowan aren't coming back.

Grandma and Grandpa do all the housework—they cook us dinner, they clean the dishes, they make Dad's bed really nice for him so it feels like a warm welcome. They even turn on the TV for us in the living room, with a movie already waiting for us to play it. Dad and I sit alone with Pumpkin in the living room and start watching *The Lord of the Rings*. It's one of our favorite movies to watch—Rowan always thought he was too cool for fantasy, and Mom said Tansy was too young to watch such violent things.

I miss them. I miss them so much, and I hate myself for spending the past fifteen years eager to grow up and move out and start my life, because now that they're gone, I realize they were my life.

"What are you thinking about?" Dad asks. The thoughts must be apparent on my face.

I shrug. "Not much." I have to try very hard to keep the words inside my mouth. I have so many questions for him I'm bursting and at any moment they all might come tumbling out. I could create a whole list of them if I wanted.

Dad, have you always been sad?
Did this just push you over the edge?

Did you really want to kill yourself?
Were you really suicidal?
Should I be as sad as you?
Am I grieving wrong?
Is there a wrong way to grieve?
Why did you keep walking after I sat down in that bush?
What would Mom think of that?
And what in the world were you looking for out there?

Instead I say, "I've seen this movie a thousand times," and change the channel.

Dad says, "You can never get tired of Frodo and Sam."

"Hanna says that *The Lord of the Rings* is too male-dominated."

"Yeah, sure it is. But that doesn't mean it can't be good. Come on, this was always our thing—*The Lord of the Rings* late at night. Do you have to listen to everything Hanna says?"

"Sometimes it feels like it."

Dad laughs. I switch it back to *The Lord of the Rings* because I can tell that he wants me to, and he smiles. "That's better."

I wonder if he has explanations on the tip of his tongue, just like how I have questions on the tip of mine. Maybe that's what it's going to be like for the two of us now—questions and answers that are never spoken aloud.

"Your mom loved these movies too, you know."

"I remember." I don't want Mom and Tansy and Rowan to become taboo topics like people seem to turn into when they die. I don't want Dad and me to choke over our words every time their names are mentioned. I want their names to float around in the air always so it feels like they haven't left.

"Rowan thought they were boring," he says.

"Rowan had terrible taste in movies."

Dad laughs and sniffs at the same time, still staring at the screen. "You're not wrong." We lapse back into uncomfortable silence, the questions still floating in the air around us like Mom, Rowan, and Tansy's ghosts.

"Dad?" I ask, deciding I'm going to let one of the questions slip out, one of the ones I can't help myself from saying. "Have...have you been sad for a long time?"

He doesn't say anything back, which makes me think maybe the answer is yes. Maybe he's been sad since before everything happened to our family and this was the thing that pushed his sadness to the point of no return.

His answer—or lack thereof—hurts so much that I say, "I'm going to bed," and I leave him downstairs. I retreat into my room and call Hanna on FaceTime, biting my cheek really hard to keep the tears from pouring out. Once they start, I won't be able to stop them. And even though I don't mind crying, sometimes opening the floodgate is too daunting. I mostly don't want Dad to hear me because he was just in the hospital and I'm afraid I'll make him run away again.

It's messed up. It's so messed up that I'm thinking that.

"Is everything OK?" Hanna asks.

"Not really."

Within an hour, Hanna and Lyssa come over. They borrow my pajamas and sleep in my bed and don't ask any questions because at this point, there are so many things hurting that they know there doesn't have to be a specific reason why. Hanna cries and I let a few tears fall and Lyssa plays music on the ukulele my mom bought me, which I never learned to use. I don't want her to stop playing because I'm afraid I'll hear my dad downstairs and he'll be crying. I wonder how many times I didn't hear him crying before. Grandpa brings us hot chocolate, even though it's summer and eighty degrees outside. We drink it up and it makes us sweat through our pajamas.

"You guys can't leave me," I tell them in between sips.

"Never," Hanna says.

"Never, ever," Lyssa adds.

I worry because Hanna might leave me if she learns how I feel about her, but I see the look on her face, her eyes sparkling with determination and loyalty and tears, and I know she's telling the truth. Maybe some things happen to people that are so terrible it makes them forget about the little things that felt big at one point because there are more important things to worry about. Maybe some things happen that are so terrible people have to make a choice—to stay or to leave. Hanna and Lyssa are going to stay.

I start crying—like real crying—and Hanna hugs me and says, "Oh, Laurel," which makes me cry more. And Lyssa says, "It's OK, we're here." Eventually I fall asleep, because even though I don't like to admit it, Grandma was right. I needed to sleep in a proper bed.

"We're going to use a Ouija board." Lyssa is standing on my front step holding an old, battered board-game box against her side and wearing a large grin on her face.

"What do you think you're doing?"

She glances down at the box in her arms and then raises her eyebrows. "Come on," she says. "Hanna is at her SAT class. I have the day off work. You're not doing anything—besides, you know, grieving."

"I don't know, Lyssa. My schedule is pretty full. I'm supposed to start moping around my bedroom at noon, and then I'm booked with feeling sad for the rest of the evening."

She laughs and I laugh too. "Come on."

"To where?"

"Well we can't do it in one of our houses! What if the spirits come out and like, latch onto your old creepy dolls?"

That makes me laugh really hard. Mom used to collect dolls. Rowan told her it was creepy because they looked haunted, and she would just say, "Good! I hope they're haunted! Then the spirits will be nicer to me than you are!" And Rowan would roll his eyes and I would laugh and Tansy would hug Mom and say, "I'm nice to you!" and Mom would say, "Yes, of course you are."

The memory makes me jump, just slightly, and Lyssa asks, "Spooked already?"

"I feel like I've been living in a permanent state of spooked for the past few weeks."

"Oof."

Lyssa and I walk to the forest behind my house. Lyssa tells me she would prefer to play with the board at the allegedly haunted house that's infamous among the students at our high school, but Lyssa can't drive on her own yet and neither can I. It's a blessing in disguise because I definitely don't want to go to a haunted house.

"Here is good," she says, sitting down on an overturned log just far enough away from the neighborhood that we can barely make out the outline of houses. She sets the box on the ground and slowly lifts out the board. It has a bunch of letters on it, with the large words "YES" and "NO" printed in circles. She places a looking glass in the middle of the board.

"You have to put your finger on it," she says. "It only works if you have two people playing."

Reluctantly, I place my finger on the looking glass, which is cold against my fingers.

Lyssa clears her throat, takes a dramatically loud, deep breath, and says, "Are there any spirits here?" The looking glass doesn't move.

"You're holding it still," she says.

"Why would I do that?"

"I don't know. Because you're a nonbeliever."

"Not true. Hanna's the nonbeliever."

"Whatever."

And it still doesn't move, no matter what Lyssa tries. Eventually, she says, "It works best with three people. The times I've used it, and it's worked, I've had at least three. One person is supposed to be the medium and ask questions, while the other two touch the glass. That's probably why it's not moving right now. We need another person; I've confused the spirits." It's almost comical how seriously Lyssa takes this stuff—it reminds me of Mom.

I suggest we ask Hanna to be the third person, and then we both burst out laughing before Lyssa even has a chance to respond. Hanna would never want to play with a Ouija board—if Lyssa thinks I might be a nonbeliever, then Hanna is on a whole other level of nonbelieving. Hanna doesn't even believe in soulmates. She says love is more about societal expectations and timing, which makes me wonder if she's ever been in love—which, consequently, makes me sad.

Mom used to warn me not to play with Ouija boards. She told me that one time, when she was a kid, she asked the board if she would die early and it flipped out and spun around the room and Mom was completely terrified to leave the house for two weeks.

Maybe Mom was always destined to die early. Rowan and Tansy too.

Lyssa and I trudge back to the house with the overwhelming feeling of disappointment, like we've come up short because we've failed at talking to spirits through a board game. Mom always said she could talk to spirits. When my grandma on Mom's side died, Mom claimed that a part of my grandma's soul latched onto hers. Dad joked that Mom couldn't be so sure because she'd already been turning into her own mother for years. He joked that Tansy and I would turn into Mom eventually too.

"Do you think we could have talked to them?" I ask her.

She frowns. "I don't know. It depends if they're sticking around in the spiritual realm or not."

"How can you tell?"

She shrugs. "I don't know. I'll read up on it and get back to you." She pauses for a few moments, like she's deep in thought, and then continues, "Ghosts usually reach out when they have something to tell you. Something unfinished. That's my theory. After my mom died, I heard her voice for years until the court ruled I officially couldn't see my dad anymore and then her voice went away. I think she was watching out for me."

If Hanna were here, she would have to physically restrain herself from commenting. Lyssa told us that she used to see her mom's ghost years ago. Hanna said that it was probably just a coping mechanism and not actually a ghost, and then Lyssa got so mad she broke Hanna's phone by throwing it across the room at a wall.

"I felt my mom. Tansy and Rowan too. At least I think I did." I don't think I did—I know I did—but I play it down a bit because I'm not sure how to explain what I saw or felt.

She nods in response.

"But I don't know what they want to tell me."

"Well, whatever it is, they'll figure out a way to tell you. I have a medium I could recommend to you. It's pricey, but I saved up babysitting money and did it once and it was really helpful. Her name is Diana, or Dina, or something like that."

Ghost Mom is jumping with joy next to me. Mom always wanted to see a medium but she said she was too afraid that her mother's spirit would say something rude and offend the medium, so she shied away.

"Maybe," I say.

We reach my doorstep, with its pots full of plants beginning to droop and the bright green paint on the door chipping slightly at the sides. "Do you think your dad is going to be OK?" she asks. Her voice is much softer now. This is a skill both she and Hanna excel at: when things get serious, their voices get soft. I don't think that's something I'm particularly good at—when things get serious, my voice runs away.

"Yes," I say.

"Me too."

I don't think either of us believes it, but sometimes all you can do is say things you don't believe because you want them to be true.

Dad is in the hospital again. He tried to overdose on Tylenol. It turns out that Tylenol is one of the most difficult drugs to overdose on because it takes so long to kill you, and he didn't swallow enough pills to do permanent damage. Grandma knocked the bathroom door down when she realized how long he'd been in there. He was still alive and breathing but sick to his stomach. So, they took him to the hospital and they're pumping his stomach. I overheard Grandma talking to a doctor about transferring him somewhere else. I don't know how to feel about that. It makes me angry, though I know I shouldn't be because everyone is just trying to help Dad get better.

But what if there is no better? What if this is our new normal, our new standard?

I wonder what it would be like to find your grown-up son on the bathroom floor with a bottle of Tylenol spilled all over the sink. I'm glad I didn't find him. I can say that because he's OK and it's not like me finding him would have made a life-saving difference—it would have only hurt me more.

The apologetic nurse sees me and smiles, not bothering with an "I'm sorry" this time. I sink down into my chair at Dad's side, hoping if I slouch low enough, I'll become invisible to the world.

Grandpa says, "Let's go get some food, Laurel." I don't want food, but I don't want any more nurses or doctors to see me and feel bad for me, so I go with him.

Hospital food isn't terrible. It's not good, but it isn't terrible. Slightly dry, but better than Grandma and Grandpa's cooking, if I'm being honest.

We eat mashed potatoes and steamed vegetables and Grandpa talks to me about how his favorite football team is looking. Even though I don't care about football, I like listening to him. It's one of the first conversations I've had since the accident that isn't dripping with memories of Mom, Rowan, and Tansy.

"We just need to work on the defensive line," he says. "Then they could win."

"I thought you said the defensive line was good."

"No, no, it was good last year. It's going to stink this year."

"Ah."

"We'll see who they pick in the first round of the draft."

It's not even football season yet and he can still talk about it for the entirety of our lunch. That's something I like about Grandpa—he knows when to talk and when not to, and what not to talk about. I should make a list of things not to talk about and make the topic of my dead family number one. I've never been one for holding in feelings. Mom always said I was brimming with emotions despite my valiant efforts to hide them, but right now it feels like there are too many feelings to talk about, so I guess it's time I really hone in on my ability to hold emotions in. Rowan was always good at that. I wish he was around to teach me a thing or two.

Rowan. He's on The List, definitely on The List. I'm also adding being in love with Hanna to The List of Things Not to Talk About with Laurel. Along with Dad being hospitalized and me going back to school in September. That's already five things. This is gonna be a long list.

I snap back to reality when I notice Grandpa has finally changed the subject to something that isn't football. "Have you told your friends about this? You could invite them over tonight."

"Sure," I say, trying my hardest not to broach one of the subjects on my list (see "Dad being hospitalized," number four).

"Your dad will probably have to stay here overnight, kiddo."

He's breached the unspoken agreement—he's chucked The List out the door without even knowing it. I stare at my mashed potatoes and run my fork through them like I'm raking a pile of dirt, making nice, straight lines like I'm in Mom's zen garden.

"Your grandma and I were talking to the nurse and he thinks it would be a really good idea if your dad were to go stay somewhere for a while, somewhere with care designed for this kind of grief, sort of like a camp but—"

"But a mental institution?"

Grandpa winces. "No, honey. Not like that."

I continue to rake patterns into my potatoes, an entire universe of squiggles and lines.

"There's a facility in Kentucky for people who are experiencing intense grief. For people in very similar situations, losing family members to traumatic accidents and, you know, the like."

Grandpa is breaking nearly every single rule on my list, which I have yet to write down somewhere. Maybe if I write it down and print copies, then everyone will take it seriously and this will never happen again.

"Kentucky is all the way across the country," I say.

"We think insurance will cover this place."

"But Kentucky is all the way across the country." My voice cracks. I don't want my voice to crack. Ghost Mom whispers in my ear, "My sweet Pisces child. Cry if you need to. Feel." I want to kick her, though I don't think it's possible to kick a ghost.

"I know. It won't be for long, Laurel."

"But I'm here."

"I know."

"Across the country." I repeat it so he understands how absolutely terrible the suggestion is.

"This place is doing really great things for people suffering from severe losses, Laurel. We think it would really help your dad. He hasn't been…your dad. He can't be your dad when he's hurting like this."

Severe loss. Those two words don't cut it—they don't even get close to describing it.

"What am I supposed to do?" I ask him. "I'm here. He can't go all the way across the country. He can't leave me."

"We'll stay here with you, of course."

"What if I'm hurting just as much and I can't be a daughter? Or a granddaughter? Or whatever I am?"

"Laurel…"

"Will you send me away, then, too?"

"Laurel, your dad thinks this is a good idea."

"Yeah, well, he also thought overdosing on Tylenol was a good idea." I gasp after the words escape my mouth. I'm crying now—not a lot, just a few drops running down my cheek. My eyes are full of water, so I keep them glued open because if I blink, more tears will pour out. I don't want that—not right now in the stupid hospital cafeteria. Grandpa tries to reach an arm out to comfort me, but I pull myself away.

"I'm going to go outside," I say.

"OK."

Outside the sunlight is blinding and I wipe the tears off my face like they're beads of sweat. I pace back and forth, daring anyone who walks by to question me. Hanna. I need to call Hanna. That's what I do when I'm upset. I call Hanna.

"Laurel? What's going on?"

"Do you have paper?"

"I—yes…what's going on?"

"I need you to make a list."

"What?"

"Call it—Things Not to Talk About with Laurel."

"I don't think this is the best idea. Where are you?"

"Please."

"Not healthy," she quips back, as if she's an expert on healthy behavior.

"My dad is at the hospital again."

"Oh…oh, Laurel."

A pause.

"I'll come and meet you. I'm so sorry, I'll pick up Lyssa and—"

"Number one," I say. "Is saying sorry. No saying sorry to me."

"What? I…"

"Please."

"Oh…fine. OK. I'm writing your list. But you know I don't think this is—"

"Healthy. I know. How about number two is my coping mechanisms."

I can practically hear her rolling her eyes.

"Number three—my family. Number four—my dad trying to kill himself. Number five—going back to school in September. Number six—you kissing me."

Hanna doesn't say anything for a few seconds. The tension in the air crackles even though she's not physically near me and we're just talking on the phone. Then she says, "Laurel, I…"

"It's not like you were talking about it anyways."

"Are you OK? We're…we're coming to see you, right now. I'm getting in the car."

"Number seven—asking me if I'm OK. Obviously, I'm not. That shouldn't even be a question. Do I sound OK? Would you be OK if you were me?"

"I'm getting in my car right now, and I'm coming."

"Aren't you supposed to be writing my list?"

"Can't write while driving."

"You don't have your license."

"I'm a better driver than half the people I know with licenses. I've got my permit. Mom'll understand." Her mom will certainly not understand, as her mom loves rules just as much as Hanna does, but I don't say anything. Silence falls between us, but neither of us hangs up. Tears openly stream down my face. An older woman approaching the hospital door with a walker tries to ask me if I'm OK.

"Don't ask me that! It's on my List of Things Not to Talk About!"

The woman stares at me like I'm crazy. I can just imagine what Rowan would do if he were here. He would gape at me because talking back to an old lady I've never met before is very out of character for me, and then he would laugh and say, "Didn't know you had it in you, sis." Growing up, he always told me I was too polite and boring and complacent and I would retort, "At least people actually like me because I'm nice, and not because they're afraid of me," and then he would aim a kick at me under the table. People were afraid of Rowan. I was afraid of Rowan sometimes. When Ghost Rowan gets near me I shiver, even though I love and miss him. He always seemed angry, and I wonder if he died angry, sitting there in the front seat of Mom's neon-blue car with a frown on his face. He wasn't always angry as a kid. It was like a switch flipped when he grew up.

"'Sup." Lyssa's voice comes through the phone, and I picture her having just climbed into the front seat of Hanna's car. Hanna, who is now a law-breaking illegal driver, all because of me. I feel bad for being kind of mad at her.

"Lyssa!" I say, "Will you obey The List?"

"The List?"

"She made me start writing this for her," Hanna says.

"You didn't finish writing number five."

"It's because she didn't like number six," I say.

Hanna groans and says, "No, it's because I got worried and decided to come see you! Now, stop distracting me while I'm *illegally* driving, please!"

"What was number six?"

"Please! Be quiet!"

For a second I get scared because I remember what happened to Mom and Rowan and Tansy while they were driving. They weren't even driving distracted. The truck was driving distracted and they still got killed. What messed-up luck would that be, for my two best friends to die in a car crash too. The universe can't be that awful. At least—I want to believe that.

Within ten minutes Hanna's car rolls up and she and Lyssa get out and run up to me. They both hug me and Hanna says, "Please tell us what happened."

"My dad took too much Tylenol."

"On purpose?" Lyssa asks.

"I don't think a person can accidentally consume so much Tylenol the doctors have to pump their stomach."

"Oh, Laurel," Hanna says. They cling to me like I'm a life raft and we're all floating at sea. Except to me they're the life rafts and I'm the sea, rocking and throwing them from side to side.

"I'm sorry," I whisper.

"Don't be," Hanna says.

"We're sorry," Lyssa says.

"You're not allowed to say that. It's on The List."

The three of us laugh—even though The List is still something I'm considering implementing for the good of us all. We walk back into the hospital. Hanna flashes me a look like she wants to say something but can't think of how to say it, so I say, "If it's on The List, we don't need to talk about it." She bites her lip and nods even though tears glisten in her eyes, and I wonder what all that might mean for us.

10

Lyssa and Hanna wait for me in the hospital lounge while I stand in the doorway of Dad's room, trying to blend into the background and catch the tail end of my grandparents' conversation.

"Maybe we should just move here. Permanently," Grandma says.

"But you're happy in Phoenix," Grandpa responds.

"I won't be happy knowing my son is…like this." Grandma's voice quivers. "If we sold the house, we could get some extra savings."

"We can afford it, you know," Grandpa says back. "Insurance covers most of it. We'll just chip in a little."

"Thousands of dollars is *not* just a little, Rubin."

"It's for the best."

"We should sell the house," Grandma says, after a moment of silence.

"We'll talk about it later tonight."

Dad is asleep. He's always asleep when he's in the hospital. It's like when he passes through the doors his body finally relaxes enough for him to sleep all the hours he's been missing out on at home. I want to say it's because he feels safe, but I know it's most definitely the drugs they give him.

"Laurel," Grandma and Grandpa say in unison when they notice me. "We were just talking about—"

"Is Dad going away?"

Grandpa frowns and Grandma nods, which means yes. Grandpa wants to sugarcoat it, but Grandma will tell it to me straight, all sour and no sweet.

"When?" I ask.

"We're working on arranging flights, but we're hoping to get him there by next week. I've already talked to the facility. They have an opening and we expressed how—well—unique his case is. And urgent."

"Can I go with him?"

"I don't think you need that right now."

"No, I don't mean like, staying there. I'm not going to make you pay for that. I mean, can I fly with him? Can I fly down with him to wherever you're shipping him off to?"

Grandma grimaces like she's about to lecture me for accusing them of shipping him off, but Grandpa speaks before she has a chance. "That's a good idea. And you can fly back on your own! Have you ever flown on your own? It's fun—I think it's fun."

"I haven't."

I've only ever flown with my entire family in tow, but now they're all dead or suicidal.

We would always get into arguments at airports, and I'm convinced that airports make people a hundred times angrier than usual. Rowan would usually mouth off at my mom about something, then Dad would tell Rowan to stop being a jerk, then Tansy would start crying and make a big deal of it, and I would slip away into the corner and wait in one of those uncomfortable airport chairs until they all calmed down.

I remember when we were going to visit my grandparents in Arizona, I sat there watching the planes take off and made up stories in my head about where they were going. I envisioned myself on one of those planes one day, going to college somewhere far away like London or Paris. But Mom had interrupted my fantasizing, sitting next to me and patting me on the knee, saying, "I'm sorry we fight so much."

And I asked, "Why are you apologizing to me about it?"

She squeezed my shoulder and said, "Because. You're the one who fights the least. You're the one who picks up the pieces."

That's what I'm doing right now, picking up all the pieces. There are too many pieces to pick up. My arms can't hold all of them—not for long. Even if Grandma, Grandpa, Lyssa, and Hanna all help me, we won't be able to clean everything up. Some things will just stay broken.

Grandpa books the plane tickets when we get home: a one-way ticket for my dad and a round trip for me. Surprisingly, they let Dad come home with us. He's stable now and we have a plan for getting him treatment, so they pounced on the opportunity to open up another bed and send him home. Plus, I heard Grandma telling Grandpa she didn't think insurance would cover another night in the hospital. Grandma didn't want me to hear that, so I pretended not to.

Grandma and Grandpa have been watching Dad like hawks, not leaving his side for more than five minutes at a time. Dad looks empty and broken, so much so that I can't bring myself to look him in the eyes because I'm afraid I'll start crying or I'll get mad at him or—even worse—I won't recognize him. Mom always said I was soft like Dad. Does that mean I'm going to be sent away too if I let the softness get the best of me?

"Do you want some soup, Laurel?" Grandpa asks me. The soup doesn't look very good—Grandpa's always been a terrible cook, though not as terrible as Grandma—but I say yes because he has this look in his eyes that tells me he's about to break. Like me, he's just barely holding it all together. I've never seen Grandpa look like that. Dad takes soup too and lifts it to his lips, barely sipping any.

"You need to eat, Quinton."

"I am." When Grandpa turns away, he feeds a spoonful to Pumpkin underneath the table. I scratch him behind the ears—I'm sure he's confused. Everyone has been so in and out the past few days, and Hanna is the one who feeds him, and maybe he's finally realized that Mom, Rowan, and Tansy aren't coming home.

I eat all of the soup, even though it looks like muddy water and tastes like it has way too much garlic in it. "Good girl, Laurel," Grandma says, like I'm the dog. As if my dad and I are both the dogs and they're just dog sitting us until our owners get back. But it turns out Mom was our owner and she's not coming back. What are we going to do without her?

"I'm going to sleep down here tonight," Dad says, as if it's a one-night thing. He's been sleeping downstairs every day since the accident, excluding the few nights he slept in the hospital and the few days he was missing. He can't bring himself to sleep upstairs in the bed he and Mom used to share. It probably still smells like her—flowers and dirt mixed with a hint of perfume and strawberry-scented shampoo.

"I'll sleep down here too."

Grandma and Grandpa protest, but then they give in because they look so tired, with more bags under their eyes than I ever thought possible. I hate going upstairs to sleep now, anyways.

They leave the two of us alone in the living room as the sky outside darkens. Neither of us makes a move for the remote—he just pulls a blanket over himself in the armchair and I tuck my knees into my chest on the couch, curled up like a little ball.

"I'm sorry," Dad says. His voice sounds distant, like it doesn't belong to him anymore.

"Don't," I tell him.

"I just...I'm so sorry."

"I made a list," I blurt out.

"What?"

"The List of Things Not to Talk About with Laurel. Saying sorry is on there. Number one, I think. That's what I told Hanna to write down first."

"Ah."

"No more saying sorry."

"OK." Dad looks like he's about to cry. "I'm going to get better," he says, his voice quiet like a whisper. "For you."

I'm not sure what to say to that. Is that something I thank him for? Or do I just say "OK"?

"I think I've been sad for a long time," he continues. "And I think…I think it's time I get help."

"How long?" I ask. "Since—since before?"

He nods.

"But you're going to a place for people grieving."

"I am grieving."

"But you said you've been sad for a long time."

"Yes."

"So you're going there for depression."

"Both."

Silence.

"I've realized," he says. "That when grief and depression team up, it's a recipe for self-destruction."

I don't think I quite understand. "That's on The List."

"What?"

"You trying to kill yourself. Self-destruction. Any reference to you trying to kill yourself counts on The List."

"Oh."

Dad starts crying softly. I say, "I'm staying down here but I don't want to talk about all those things with you. OK?"

"OK." He sniffs and chuckles softly. "I'm going to need a copy of that list." I'm glad he doesn't tell me it's not a healthy coping mechanism like Hanna did.

After a while Dad turns on the TV, because neither of us can fall asleep easily anymore, and we watch reruns of *Friends*. Dad cries because Phoebe always reminded him of Mom, but he doesn't say anything out loud because he respects The List. I know why he's crying though, so I try and make a mental list of all the ways Phoebe is not like Mom. Mom wasn't blonde, for starters. She had red hair, and she wasn't tall—she was pretty short. And she definitely wasn't a cat person; she thought cats were too spiteful.

When I feel myself drifting off, I whisper, "Dad?"

"Hmm?"

"Please don't try to kill yourself tonight." The fear is bubbling up in my stomach, telling me to keep my eyes open at all times.

"You're breaking your own rules," he says. His voice is thick, like my words have sliced through him and opened him up and now he's bleeding all over the couch.

"I know. I just wanted to tell you that. Because I'll be really mad at you if you do."

"I won't," he says. "I'll be OK. Promise."

I wonder if that means I'll be OK too. Mom always said Dad and I were the same. "You're both water signs," she would say. Rowan hated how much Mom talked about astrology. One time, he told her she was stupid for believing in it and she told him he wasn't allowed to talk like that to his mother. Dad got mad at Rowan, and Tansy cried, and I disappeared. It was our family ritual.

I want to ask Dad what he was looking for on the trail. I've been wanting to ask him ever since he came back, but I've been afraid of the answer. In my half-asleep state, I start packing up the courage to ask, but then I hear Dad snore softly. I guess it's too late to ask him, at least tonight. Alone, I stare at the TV and continue to think of all the ways Phoebe from *Friends* is not like Mom. I fall asleep doing that.

11

Less than a week after Dad came home, I'm sitting in my bedroom packing for a trip to drop him off in Kentucky.

The weird thing about somebody you know being sent away to a camp for sad adults (one of the *many* weird things) is that they have to go through the entire process of getting there. They have to pack a bag, go to the airport, and sit on a plane next to their family, or friends, or a complete stranger, and stare out the window while knowing they're not going on a fun vacation—instead, they're going to a camp for sad adults, or rather, a glorified mental institution. There was a kid at my middle school who got sent away to a rehab facility in Denver. Everyone said it was because she was doing cocaine, but I heard it was actually because she was suicidal. Not sure what the truth is, but I never once thought about her going to the facility. I just imagined she appeared there one day, or they carted her off in a private jet to get there as soon as possible. But if her situation was anything like Dad's, she had to get on a plane full of people going on vacation or visiting family and be very aware of the fact that she was not going anywhere particularly fun.

Hanna comes over to help me pack, which doesn't take much effort, as it's just throwing an extra shirt and some books into a backpack. I think it's just an excuse to come over and try to clear up the awkward tension that arose between us when I brought up the kiss. She tells me she's sorry, despite the fact that this technically breaks the rules of The List, and I tell her I'm sorry too, though neither of us says exactly what we're apologizing for. We flit around the subject like it's made of broken glass and we might cut ourselves.

"Is that OK? To say sorry? I think I broke the rules of your list." She gives me a slight smile, which I return.

"I'll let that one slide. Besides, the saying-sorry rule applies more to, well, my family."

She nods and chews on her lip. "I'll respect your list. No more sorry from now on."

"You…you don't have to. It's fine," I say, though deep down, it means a lot that she wants to respect it, and I'm mostly just saying that because I don't want to fight—I don't have the energy left for that.

"Do you think this will help your dad?" she asks while sitting on the ground and tossing a pair of socks into my backpack.

"I don't know."

"I think it will." I can tell that she's saying it more for her than for me, because sometimes, we have to say things to believe in them.

The website calls this place a "Wellness Center for the Bereaved," but that just sounds like a fancy way of saying "Sad Camp in The Middle of Nowhere, Kentucky." It's decorated with pictures of flowers and cabins drenched in sunlight, smiling people with their arms around one another. Mom would have gotten a kick out of Dad going to a place like that.

In the morning, Hanna's mom drops Dad and me off at the airport—him with all his luggage and me with my measly backpack. Grandma and Grandpa don't like to drive on the freeway, so Mrs. Jackson offered to take Dad and me so that they could rest. Grandma protested at first but then said, "Oh, fine, OK," and kissed me on the cheek and then fell asleep on the couch with Pumpkin on her lap. Grandpa smirked at her and thanked Mrs. Jackson for driving us. And suddenly, the five of us (me, Dad, Hanna, Mrs. Jackson, and Lyssa, who came along for the ride) are standing in the airport saying goodbye.

"You take care of yourself," Mrs. Jackson says to Dad.

"He won't be taking care of himself," I say. "Other people will."

Mrs. Jackson frowns at me, Lyssa laughs, and Hanna shakes her head. Dad just looks broken, like he's not really here, like he's secretly living in an alternate universe.

"You text us when you land, and keep us posted on your return flight information. We'll see you tomorrow morning." I'm supposed to stay at an airport hotel overnight that Grandpa booked for me, and then I'm flying back home at six in the morning the next day.

"I will."

Mrs. Jackson nods and then tells us we'd better get to the gate. Hanna and Lyssa say goodbye, Hanna gives Dad a hug, and Lyssa pats him on the back like they're old pals or something.

"See you in a few weeks, Pops!" Lyssa calls. Hanna shakes her head and laughs, and then they're gone.

I'm not sure if it will be a few weeks. A few weeks is what Grandpa told me, but we haven't booked Dad's return flight yet, so I guess it's just going to be as long as it takes for him to get better. There's not much that can be done to make him better. Mom and Rowan and Tansy are all dead; I don't think there's anything we can fix.

Dad tries to act like everything is OK, like we're going on a family trip with what's left of our family. Except I notice that when we pass the airport Hudson store, his eyes get watery, because Mom used to always like to stop at those stores to buy gum. She said chewing gum helped pop her ears on the plane.

"Want anything?" Dad asks.

"No," I say, mostly because I don't want the two of us to start crying in the middle of an airport Hudson store over a pack of gum.

Mom was right—Dad and I are the two watery ones. We'll cry over anything, although I have been trying my best not to cry lately, or at least not to make a big deal of my crying. Without Mom and Rowan and Tansy, the two of us are going to drown in our own tears.

Ghost Tansy really wants me to sit near the window in the airport so we can watch planes on the runway. So, Dad and I pick seats near the window when we get to our gate. I don't tell Dad about Ghost Tansy prompting me though. Even if he's felt them hanging around too—I want to keep them to myself.

Hours pass. Since the accident, I've gotten pretty good at letting time slip through the cracks. What used to take forever seems like only a couple of minutes now. We board the plane and I let Dad slide in first so he can rest against the window. I've always been used to the middle seat anyways. Rowan and Tansy always made me sit in the middle. Dad and Mom would sit in front of us and when we were really young, we'd kick at their chairs until they turned around and yelled at us on a crowded plane.

I love planes, mostly because they're a total wonder to me. We pack a bunch of humans and their luggage into giant chunks of metal and then magically send it into the air. It really shouldn't work. Humans are not supposed to fly. I've made Hanna explain planes to me hundreds of times—she loves talking about physics and why things are the way they are—but I still don't remember half of what she says. I just know planes take me places I want to go. Except this time I don't want to drop my dad off at Sad Camp in Kentucky.

We didn't get one of those nice planes with the tiny screens in front of each seat, so I have to pull out a book and try to read. The words feel too difficult to process right now, so instead I just lean back and stare at the ceiling of the plane. All the buttons and the three tiny lights that are pointing at me, Dad, and the lady sitting to my right. The flight is full, which is weird to me, because I didn't think a flight to Louisville, Kentucky, would be full on a Wednesday morning. What if everyone else on here is also going to Sad Camp? The thought makes me laugh, and the lady next to me gives me an odd look before drifting off to sleep in her likely overpriced neck pillow. I've never thought neck pillows were very comfortable; they mostly just make my neck hurt, and they're sweaty.

Ghost Tansy is excited about flying—I can feel the nervous excitement in her stomach in my toes and my fingers, as if she's sending the feelings from her body, or lack thereof, to mine. She was ten (almost eleven) when she died, but she always acted like she was five years younger than her age. Rowan called it "youngest child syndrome," and Mom said it was because she had a young spirit. Dad and I always laughed at her and shook our heads, keeping our lips sealed.

Maybe Dad and I are the ones left behind because we never said much. I know Hanna would tell me I'm being silly and it doesn't work like that, but it sort of feels like the world is punishing us for being too quiet, or maybe the world is punishing Mom and Rowan and Tansy for being too loud, for taking up so much space that the world had no choice but to shut them out. Rowan and his booming voice and all his soccer friends, Tansy and her excited squeals on Christmas morning and the bright-colored bows she liked to wear in her hair, Mom and her colorful pants and how she liked to talk to plants because she said their spirits could hear us. Dad and I are the boring ones—Dad and his books, me and my daydreaming.

Thinking about them forms a knot in my throat, so instead I turn my attention to trying to pop my ears (without the help of chewing gum, which I refused to buy from the Hudson), stare at the ceiling, and eventually close my eyes until the voice comes over the loudspeaker and tells us to prepare for landing. Dad doesn't move from his sleep, not even when the flight attendant asks him to put his seat in an upright position, and he doesn't even wake up when I push his seat up for him. He snores softly and looks so peaceful. It makes me want to never get off the plane and let him stay here forever.

Over the course of the car ride, I learn even more about Sad Camp. Dad rambles on and on about the facilities and amenities as we pass by rolling green hills and empty highways. Apparently, he's sleeping in one of the three large log cabins at the camp, which are fully equipped with nice beds, Wi-Fi, and in-cabin laundry. Dad seems particularly excited about the laundry part.

The sun shines on me in the front seat of the car and I'm already sweating, the humidity and heat opening all my pores for the world to see. Dad keeps nodding his head and saying that he'll make some lifelong friends here, though I'm pretty sure that's just his way of trying to make me feel better, trying to make it seem like this is all a perfectly normal thing for a father and daughter to do together.

"Very sad lifelong friends," I mutter. The car pulls off the highway and we slow down as the log cabins come into view. They're certainly not as beautiful as they looked on the website, but they definitely have charm. The cab driver parks and nods at my dad, who thanks him awkwardly before climbing out of the seat beside me.

Above the entrance to the largest building, it says "Charles Sanctuary for the Recently Bereaved" in large letters. I can't help but wonder who Charles is, or was. Probably was, since it's a place for people who are seeing ghosts. I mean, at least one person there has to be seeing or feeling ghosts. Otherwise I must be abnormal, and I might be the one who belongs here instead of Dad.

When we step inside, I'm surprised to see that the interior resembles a hotel much more than a log cabin—bright lighting and the smell of cleaner fluid. There are flowers everywhere, beautiful decorations trying to convince everyone this is a place for happiness instead of a place for sad people.

A man ushers us over to a desk that sits in the middle of the entrance. There, a lady with a large, toothy smile shakes our hands and has Dad fill out a bunch of paperwork. She looks at me and asks, "Are you his daughter?"

I nod. It should be obvious—I've always been told I look just like Dad, and nothing like Mom. Mom passed along most of her appearance to Tansy and Rowan, and none of them are left. Maybe it was Mom who was cursed. The thought makes me shiver, despite the humidity in the wooden cabin.

"And you're here by yourself?" she asks me.

"I'm with him."

"But you're going back by yourself?"

"Yes, ma'am."

"How old are you?"

"Fifteen."

"By yourself? Wow. That's a long trip."

"Almost fifteen and a half."

Counting half birthdays feels silly, like it's something I'm too old for, but every August I still buy myself a cupcake on my half birthday. Mom instilled the tradition in me. She once celebrated Tansy's quarter birthday, which was pretty funny.

The woman nods and then tells me to ask if I need anything and to give them a call if I need help getting to the airport. Adults always act like they were never fifteen; I know I'm a lot younger than her, but I'm not incompetent. Also, I just lost a lot of my family and Hanna says grief can age a person. Hanna said that at the funeral after Lyssa commented that Dad looked like he'd aged years in just a week. I told Hanna that if grief ages people, then I was going to become an old lady much sooner than anticipated.

The woman behind the counter takes Dad's paperwork and smiles, then asks if we're ready to see his room. I want to shout at her that I'm not—I'd much rather take my dad away from this stale, hotel-like camp and go home. Instead, I nod and feign a smile. She offers to carry one of Dad's bags, and then we follow her out the door and along a gravel path in the blazing sunlight.

I don't like it here. All the adults keep looking at me like they're surprised I'm the one dropping Dad off because I should be accompanied by another adult. I want to tell them I don't have another adult to accompany me and I didn't want Dad to go here all by himself, and that Grandpa said going on a trip would be good for me. Maybe none of my family—or what's left of my family—really knows what we're doing anymore and yes, I'm staying in a hotel by myself and I'm kind of scared, but I also don't want people to feel bad for me.

Of course I don't say anything—I just smile at the people who give me strange looks and keep my mouth shut. I spent a lifetime watching Rowan not know how to keep his own mouth shut. For reference, one time he said to his music teacher, "You're not very good at piano, you know," and that got him a note sent home. It wasn't that big of a deal, but the music teacher got really offended because he loved piano so much and a child told him he wasn't good.

Hanna says people ramble when they're deregulating. *Deregulating.* That's a Hanna word. Lyssa would just say "going nuts." That's what I'm doing—rambling, going nuts, deregulating.

Dad is sleeping in Cabin Two, which is the Earth Cabin. Apparently, all three cabins have themes—water, earth, and air. It feels cheesy to me, but Dad gets a chuckle out of it. Inside the cabin, there are a bunch of smaller rooms, each with one to three beds all squished together closely.

Dad has a roommate, an older man called Jerry, who has wrinkles around his eyes and walks with a cane. Jerry just lost his wife, which makes me wonder whether being around a bunch of people who are missing other people would make me less sad or much sadder. "Hi," I say, and he nods at me with very sad eyes, and I wonder what Mom would do if she was here.

Mom would know what to say to him, because Mom was always good at helping people, which is why she was a therapist for a while. I remember the day she quit that job and she stormed in the door, kicked off her shoes, and said to me, "Laurel, remember this—just because you're good at something doesn't mean it's good for you." So I guess helping people wasn't good for her, but I still wonder if she could have helped Jerry, because his eyes are so sad it's hard to look at.

The woman says, "I'll let you two have some time alone," and both she and Jerry slip out of the room and leave Dad and me alone. It still feels cramped, even with just the two of us, and I wonder how he's going to do living in such close quarters with a stranger, surrounded by other strangers. I watch as Dad unloads things from his suitcase, neatly folding his shirts into a small, three-drawer end table at the foot of his bed. "You'll have to get going soon," he tells me. "I've got orientation, and your taxi is waiting for you."

It all feels very quick, and I don't know how I got here— how we got here. Eventually, he turns around to face me and I see he's crying—full-on crying now—which makes me cry. He says, "You really shouldn't have come here with me." I tell him to stop and then he says something about me staying in a hotel all night by myself. I tell him I'll send him pictures, but he shakes his head and tells me they don't allow cell phones most of the time at this place.

"Then what's the point of the Wi-Fi?" I ask.

He frowns and then lets out a laugh, deep and wet with his tears, and shrugs.

"It's like the Dark Ages here," I say, and I continue to tell him that I'll send Grandma and Grandpa pictures and have them print them and mail them to him. That makes Dad smile and wrap his arms around me.

When he hugs me, I suck up all the courage I possibly can and ask the thing that's been eating away at me since he went missing in the forest: "What were you looking for?"

He pulls away and frowns. "What?"

"When you disappeared in the forest." My voice shakes a little. I'm more nervous than I should be, because I'm afraid of the answer. "What were you looking for that was so important you left me?"

He pauses for a few breaths and then says, "A rowan tree and a tansy flower."

That makes us both really, really start crying. My throat feels like it's going to close up forever and my eyes feel like they're burning.

"They don't grow at home," I manage to tell him. He already knows this—Mom would say it all the time because Tansy would get jealous about how many laurel bushes were near our house. She would tell Tansy she'd have to drive far to see wild tansies, and same with rowan trees. She said they were special. That made Tansy feel better and me feel worse, though I never said anything about it.

"I know," Dad says, "But I thought I'd give it a try."

"Oh."

Dad starts crying harder and says things I can't make out. I hear "sorry" in there, though, which is on The List. I tell him that, but it doesn't make him stop crying or stop apologizing. Eventually, the office lady comes into Dad's room and says it's time for me to leave. So I do. I don't hug him again—we've already gotten that part out of the way, and if he puts his arms around me one more time, I'll melt into a puddle of tears. I wave goodbye and give him a smile, but Dad doesn't stop crying, and it doesn't feel like a real goodbye. Real goodbyes are supposed to happen after all the crying—at least, that's what I tell myself. They're not supposed to feel so empty.

As I move to leave the cabin, I can't help but think how this would all be very different if that stupid truck driver hadn't run a red light and smashed Mom's car to pieces. How one person messed up my family's life so bad that now here I am, dropping Dad off at a camp for grieving people, preparing to go back to a home that doesn't feel like home.

"Do you need a ride to your hotel?" the woman asks.

"My dad got a taxi driver to take me."

"OK. I'll walk you there."

As we trudge through the dirt away from the cabins and toward the taxi, leaves crunch underneath my feet. They're green and long and I would recognize them anywhere—laurel leaves. Because of course laurel bushes grow in The Middle of Nowhere, Kentucky. They haunt me wherever I go. My chest gets tight and I ball my fingers up, my fingernails digging into my palms. The taxi driver waves at me and I snap out of it, nodding at the lady from the counter as I climb into the back seat. I make sure to step on a few extra laurel leaves before I climb in, grinding and crunching them into tiny, unrecognizable pieces.

The taxi driver is waiting right where we left him. He doesn't ask any questions, which is a good thing, because I don't want to explain it all, and I especially don't want him to ask me what I've been crying about. I wonder if he has to drop people here often. I hope not, because that would mean that there were a lot of bereaved people in the world. I watch the trees go by and imagine the wheels of the car running over dozens of laurel leaves that have blown onto the road, crushing them into itty-bitty pieces, so that when I look at them, I won't recognize them, and I won't remember my mother and how she died and how naming me after such a common plant became a curse.

When the taxi driver drops me off outside the airport hotel, I stare up at it and feel like I'm going to be sick. My stomach cramps like there's a fist wrapped around it, gripping tightly. The hotel will obviously smell like hotel, and Charles Sanctuary for the Recently Bereaved smelled like hotel, and that place made me feel very sad, as if the grief from everyone there formed a giant grief monster that stuck its hands straight into my chest, cold and shaky. So instead of going into the hotel, I walk toward the airport along the concrete, the hot summer sun shining on my back. I step through the automatic sliding doors and sit outside of security in the air-conditioned building and wonder if I should sleep here.

The airport in Kentucky is small—much smaller than the ever-expanding SeaTac airport—and it's fairly empty, so maybe I'll be able to find a hidden corner where nobody will notice me. Grandpa would be upset because he paid for the hotel and even let me take his credit card with me so I would have proof that we paid. But I really, really don't want to smell hotel.

I sit with my back against the wall near the ticketing area and take my phone out of my pocket to open up Wikipedia and start researching the rowan tree. At the airport, nobody gives me strange looks. It's normal to be by yourself at an airport, and nobody knows I just spent the day dropping my dad off at Charles Sanctuary for the Recently Bereaved. I don't know how my grandparents even found this place—I guess the doctors referred them and it worked with insurance, but there must be something like this back at home so I'm not sure why we had to send him to Kentucky.

People walk by me hurriedly, tripping over their own feet to make it to their flights on time. People chatter excitedly as they hold their boarding passes and watch exhausted parents drag kids along behind them. I shake my head, forcing down the lump in my throat, and stare at the Wikipedia page on my phone.

Rowan trees are also called mountain-ashes, and they are native to the Northern Hemisphere. The name "rowan" popped up in the 1800s because it's from an Old Norse word that means "to redden," and the berries that grow from rowan trees are red, which is fitting, considering Rowan's red hair. I'm reading this all from Wikipedia and teachers at school always tell us not to use Wikipedia as a source, which I don't understand because it has a lot of information. I think they just like to make it harder for us to write reports.

Rowan trees grow natively in northern Europe and on mountains in southern Europe and Southwest Asia, which Dad should have looked up before trying to search for them in Washington. It makes me kind of mad. Of course he was looking for rowan and tansy—always Rowan and Tansy.

The tansy is a plant with leaves and yellow button-like flowers. I've always thought Tansy's name suited her. Tansies are found in all parts of Europe and also in Asia and Canada and some places in the U.S., which makes me think I should just go to Europe and get out of here and find the plants for Dad so that he'll stop looking and finally pay attention to me.

That sounds bitter. It's not like I don't want him to miss them because I understand—I miss them too. But I'm the only one who's still alive and it's like he still doesn't see me, like he never saw me, like I was always the invisible child.

I won't be able to bring a tree back from Europe. But I do have Grandpa's credit card.

He would be very mad if I used it for anything unnecessary, and a flight to somewhere I'm not supposed to be is unnecessary.

And Grandma—she would be even madder. Her face would go all red to match her hair and she'd narrow her eyes at me and ask, "Who do you think you are, Laurel Summers?"

I don't know, Grandma. But I'm trying to find out.

So maybe it is necessary. If I find a rowan tree and a tansy flower to show Dad, then he'll be better. I should call Hanna to talk about it. I dial her number and lean my head back against the hard wall that's cold from the air-conditioning.

"Hello?" Her voice sounds groggy and tired, like I've just woken her up. Or perhaps she's been groggy and tired since the accident. That's what's been happening to me.

"If I tell you something, will you promise not to tell me I'm being crazy?" Nervous jitters bubble up in my stomach.

"You know I can't make that promise." Hanna laughs. She always tells me that I'm being crazy.

"I don't think I want to come home," I admit. The words feel foreign and sour on my tongue. I can taste their selfishness the minute I speak.

"What do you mean?"

"At least, not yet. I don't want to come home."

"What…what are you going to do instead?"

I can hear the gears turning in Hanna's head. She's trying to figure me out. I bet she's already texted Lyssa while on the phone with me to tell her I'm losing it in the middle of a Kentucky airport, too far away for them to come running to my aid.

"My dad was looking for them," I tell her.

She doesn't say anything back. I don't think she knows what I'm talking about, so I clarify. "On the trail. When you found me. My dad was looking for a rowan tree and a tansy flower."

"He was looking in the wrong place," she says, not missing a beat. "Those don't grow here. At least, not natively, although I have seen some tansy flowers on the side of the road before, up near the mountains."

Hanna is a mobile library. When she met my family, she thought that it was really interesting that all three of us were named after plants, so she took it upon herself to do all the research and then tell me if she thought we fit our names. She probably didn't use Wikipedia, though, because of course she agrees with teachers on that one. She concluded Tansy was the only one who fit her name, but only time would tell because Tansy only fit her name because she was cute and vibrant and a little kid. Time didn't tell because Tansy never got to grow out of that.

"I don't think he was thinking about all that." People pass me by in the airport, not even bothering to glance my way. "He wasn't exactly in the right state of mind to know where to go to find a rowan tree or a tansy flower."

"Yes, that's probably true."

"Considering now he is officially 'unstable.'"

"He's very sick, Laurel."

"I know."

"I'm...I'm worried you are too."

I frown. I imagine myself throwing the phone across the airport when she says that—a wave of defensiveness pulses through my body, and it takes all I have not to hang up (or chuck my phone).

"I'm not going to kill myself, Hanna."

"I know that." A pause. "But grief looks very different on each person."

"Don't tell me how to grieve."

"I'm not. I'm saying that just because you don't seem as bad as your dad, that doesn't mean you're not hurting just as much."

I almost throw my phone this time, I really do. I even move it away from my ear and hold it up over my head, and a little boy walking by raises his arms over his head, like he's ready to catch it. My limbs feel jittery, like I've just drunk three cups of coffee.

"Hanna," I say, finally, after putting the phone back to my ear like nothing has happened. "What if I go to Europe?"

"Sorry?"

"I googled it."

"Did you use Wikipedia again?"

"Yes, don't lecture me."

She holds back.

"They grow there. Rowan and tansy."

"Yes, but—"

"I have my passport with me."

"You're by yourself."

"So?"

"You can't even stay in a hostel if you're under eighteen, I'm pretty sure."

"I bet I can find somewhere."

"Your grandparents would be so upset, Laurel."

I'm crying now. I don't even know where the tears come from, but people start staring at me now. They keep their distance, though, because crying is fairly commonplace at airports—airports are full of goodbyes. If it was anywhere else, someone might come up to me and ask if I'm OK, but I'm protected by the natural paradox of airports, places where it's OK to have emotions because they're filled with so much excitement and heartbreak at the same time. I'm crying loud enough that Hanna can hear me, because she says, "Laurel, hey, it's OK." And then after a few breaths she continues. "Well, if you're trying to find both rowan trees and tansy plants, the Scottish Highlands would be your best bet."

Hanna has never left the U.S., but she acts like she has because she reads about traveling so much. Hanna's mom is afraid of planes. Hanna says that once she's in college she's going to study abroad and explore the world, which is what I want to do too. I want to disappear for a while and live in places where nobody would ever expect quiet, boring Laurel Summers to live.

"And there's a flight that can get you to New York and then Edinburgh this evening. It's kind of expensive, though, but, oh, there's one with a layover in London and that's a bit cheaper…"

Hanna is a very good friend. She likes to criticize and can't stop herself from inserting her opinion, but once she sees something is wrong, she will stop criticizing and start helping. It's OK to be a critical person as long as you know when and how to stop being a critical person.

"I can book it for you," Hanna says. "If you read me your credit card info and your passport number, I can do it right now, over the phone, but only if you really want me to. Also, I don't think it's a good idea to use your grandpa's money. Really, it's not a good idea to go in the first place—but if you really want to—I'll help."

She doesn't know how to stop herself from inserting her opinion. I'm used to it by now.

"I have savings," I say.

"Oh, I know," she says. My savings were always infamous in the Summers household. Mom said that I probably still had birthday money saved from my fifth birthday. I used to keep all my cash in this gray mouse-shaped purse hidden deep in my overstuffed sock drawer, and then for my thirteenth birthday, Mom said I could get a debit card because it wasn't smart to keep all the cash in one place. "And besides," she would say, "we're trying to go paperless."

Rowan always spent all his money on trips with his friends and going to the movies, and Tansy liked to spend her money on candy and toys. For me, I always envisioned the money being something I used down the line, like when I went to college or when I moved out and became an entirely different person. I'd imagine myself strolling along the streets of Paris or somewhere with so much money saved up from birthdays over the years that it wouldn't matter how expensive my lunch was, and the exchange rate wouldn't matter either. I do feel like an entirely different person now, but not for any of the reasons I fantasized about.

But Dad hasn't been working and Grandma and Grandpa only have so much money, so I should just let the idea die like I did when I was a kid and thought about running away, or like a few weeks ago when I thought about cutting all my hair off—a fleeting act of rebellion, in one ear and out the other, only possessing me for a few seconds at a time.

"I don't know if I really want you to do that," I tell her eventually.

"That's OK."

Then, I start crying again and I can't stop, won't stop, until something soft falls at my feet. There, sitting next to my shoe after falling from the journal of a curly-haired boy hurrying toward security, is a pressed daisy.

14

The daisy flower lands on my foot and an overpowering feeling washes over me, like something very important is about to happen. I stuff my phone into my pocket and run after the boy with the journal, pushing past crowds of people and families who are all heading toward security. Someone yells something at me about being rude, but I ignore them and push on toward the boy with the journal. I follow him all the way to the middle of the security line, and when I finally catch him (he's walking very fast), I say, "Hey! Hey, you dropped something!"

He turns around and I see on his face that he probably isn't a young boy like I thought, as he has some wrinkles around his eyes and is probably in his twenties, teetering somewhere between boy and adult. His eyes widen when he sees me, most likely because there are still tears running down my cheeks, my eyes are bloodshot, and I can only assume that I look like a crazy person. Hanna's muffled voice issues from the phone in my pocket: "Laurel? Laurel, are you still there?"

I hold out the daisy toward him. It's pressed and laminated, like it could be a bookmark. He glances between my eyes and the flower and hesitates a minute before slowly reaching out to take it.

"Are…are you OK?" he asks.

"Not really." I watch him open a leather-bound journal and slide the laminated flower bookmark into it. It's full of more laminated flower bookmarks, like he's collected a garden in a journal, with pinks and yellows and greens, nearly every color of flower I could imagine. Mom would have loved it with all her heart.

"What are those for?" I ask him.

"My…one of my best friends," he says. He starts shoving the journal into his bag, which is full of other papers that nearly fall out and fly onto the floor. He just barely catches them before they scatter everywhere.

"You press flowers for your best friend?"

"Yes, and if you don't mind, I'm trying to get to my gate because she's coming home tonight for the first time in two years and if I had known before two hours ago I wouldn't have agreed to play a show out here."

"You play shows? Like, music?"

I don't stop following him as we move past the crowds of people checking their bags and follow the signs toward the security checkpoint. I feel like an eager dog, but mostly I just want to see into the journal because he might have a tansy flower or a leaf from a rowan tree. He has a guitar on his back and a rucksack, and he says he plays music, so I assume that means he's worldly or whatever.

"Yes," he says. He gets in line for security, so I do too. In front of us is a full family with three kids, two boys and a girl, and it reminds me so much of my own family that I feel the knot in my throat forming. The mom is rattling off directions to her kids and handing out passports, while the dad cleans crumbs off of the little boy's face. And then, as if to rub it all in without meaning to, the boy with the journal frowns at me and asks, "Where are your parents?"

I groan—partly because I don't want to tell this stranger where my parents are and partly because I'm tired of people asking me that. "Do I really look that young?" I ask him.

"How old are you?"

"I'm fifteen."

"Then yes."

"Ten-year-olds fly alone all the time." I'm not sure if it's true, but I feel like I need to say it to prove a point. In front of us, the mom glances back at me nervously, as if worried I'll give her kids ideas about flying on their own.

"I'm sure they do," he comments. He hasn't taken his hand out of his bag, like he's afraid the journal will jump out on its own and I'll run away with it. It's not like I could go anywhere, though—we're in line for security, packed like sardines between groups of people, and security guards stand alongside the line, waiting for something suspicious to happen.

"That's probably how the flowers fell out," I tell him.

"What?"

"You keep holding it. You were probably playing with the pages. You should just keep it deep in your bag so they don't fall out again."

He looks both annoyed and amused with me. He asks me if I have a flight to catch and I say, "Of course. I'm at an airport." I leave out the fact that my flight is in the morning and I'm supposed to be staying at a hotel tonight, because if I mention that then I'll have to explain why I'm not in the hotel, and then I'll have to explain that Charles Sanctuary for the Recently Bereaved smells like a hotel and my dad is there because the rest of my family died, and all that would certainly classify as oversharing. Plus, he looks like he needs to be somewhere. I just want to look for a tansy and a rowan.

"Can I please see your journal?"

He frowns at me. "You already saw it."

"Please? I need to find something." We shuffle along in line and the family in front of us starts taking off their jackets and shoes, preparing early.

His eyes look very kind, but he also looks very confused. I get the feeling he's one of those guys who is very good with little kids but is terrified of teenagers. I don't blame him— sometimes I'm terrified of teenagers too, and I am one.

"What's her name?"

"What?"

"Your friend. The one the flowers are for. What's her name?"

He pauses for a moment and then says, "Hailey." We're getting close to the security guard, so he takes off his jacket and checks to make sure all his liquids are in a bag. I suppose I should be doing the same, but I only have a backpack with me and it's not particularly full of liquids.

I glance at my phone and see that Hanna hung up and texted me instead saying, "Please reply." I tell her, "I'm fine, I'm just doing something important." I put my phone away so I can't see her reply because I don't want it to distract me from my mission of retrieving the flowers. The family in front of us reaches the security guard, and they hand over their boarding passes and passports.

"Why are you pressing flowers for your friend Hailey?"

"Because I haven't seen her in two years and it's kind of hard to send flowers to London."

"London? Wow." I try to envision myself living in London, all on my own, wearing fashionable clothes and carrying a briefcase. I'm not sure why I'm carrying a briefcase; I guess London Laurel is more professional than normal Laurel. I always wanted to go to London, partly because I love the accents, and partly because I want to go everywhere. But that version of Laurel—the one with the fancy clothes and the briefcase—seems much more fictional now than ever before. I can barely picture myself living normally at home with everything that's changed, let alone anywhere else.

"Are you in love with her?" I ask him. In front of us, one of the kids drops their passport and the mom drops her bag, the contents slipping out onto the floor. Behind us people are complaining, but I don't care about the holdup. Granted, my flight isn't for quite some time.

He frowns and then half smiles and says, "How did you know?"

"Is she in love with you?"

He blushes like he's also fifteen years old for a moment—it's the same deep red Rowan used to turn whenever we'd ask him about his girlfriend of the month. The boy says, "Yes, we…yes."

"I know because you've been pressing flowers for her for two years and also I have one of those best friends who I'm in love with."

"At fifteen?"

"Yup. It's confusing."

He laughs. "It gets less confusing."

"It doesn't sound like it, since she's in London and you're in an airport in Kentucky."

He looks like he's not sure whether to laugh or groan, so he makes a noise that sounds somewhere in between and then says, "Good point."

I like this. I can be more open with him because he doesn't know anything about me. He's not going to look at me with pity because he doesn't know that my whole family is either dead or in the mental hospital, with the exception of my grandparents. Thinking about my grandparents makes me feel guilty because they did pay for the hotel and now I am three groups of people away from going through security so I guess I won't be staying at the hotel, unless I impulsively run out of line and abandon my mission of looking for rowan and tansy in the flower journal.

"So, can I see it? Please?"

He shakes his head, smiles at me, and then says, "How about I show this to you after we get through this line?" And then he looks behind me, like he's looking for someone, and says, "And you're sure your parents aren't here?"

"One hundred percent." He has no idea how sad that answer is, because my mom is gone and my dad feels as good as gone, cooped up at Sad Camp in a state we'd never been to before today. At least, I don't think Dad has been to Kentucky before, but maybe he has. Parents have secret lives before their children.

The family in front of us finally moves forward, and then the boy with the journal walks up to the stand and hands over his passport and his boarding pass to the guard. He moves through quickly, and then the guard ushers me over. When she sees my boarding pass she frowns and narrows her eyes at me. "Your flight isn't for another twelve hours."

"Yes, and check-in is twenty-four hours in advance," I say.

"Alright." She narrows her eyes at me and glances at my passport. "You traveling alone?"

"Yes, ma'am."

"Go ahead."

I move through quickly, stuffing my things into one of the bins and setting it on the conveyor belt, following the gaggles of people to the line for the metal detector. After collecting my things on the other end and lacing up my shoes, I find the flower-journal boy waiting on a bench with the journal in his lap. He smiles at me and waves, then asks, "So, how long do you have until your flight?"

"Eleven hours and fifty-two minutes."

He opens his mouth like he's about to say something and then just shakes his head, as if I've already confused him enough for the day and at this point, he's chosen to accept it. "I have about forty minutes, but I bet it'll be delayed."

"What makes you say that?"

"My luck. Also, the lightning outside."

I glance at a window. He's right—it's stormy and flashes of lightning illuminate the airport in a way that's both terrifying and beautiful. The light bounces off the walls and the thunder

makes people jump. He stands and says, "My gate is this way."
I follow behind him like a kid following an older brother.

I used to follow Rowan around all the time. This guy reminds me of what Rowan would have been like if he hadn't grown up angry, because when we were kids, Rowan used to play music and joke around and maybe deep down he was romantic, even though he tried to hide it. But then he got angry, and this guy doesn't seem like the angry type. I don't know why people grow up angry; that's just what growing up does to some people. I sometimes wonder if we did something to Rowan—was it Mom's fault? Or Dad's? But I can't think of anything they could have done wrong, so maybe it was just in Rowan's blood—maybe it was completely out of our control.

As we walk, he hands me the journal. I don't even take the time to hold it and look through gently; instead, I start flipping through the pages rapidly. "What are you doing here?" he asks me. We walk past gate after gate, family after family.

"Visiting my dad." It's not a lie. I was also dropping off my dad at a camp for sad, grieving adults, but he doesn't need to know that part.

"And why do you want to look at my flowers so badly?"

"I'm looking for something."

"What?"

"Well. A tree and a flower, though some classify it as a weed, but I think those people are wrong because it's too pretty to be a weed."

He stops walking and turns to me. We're standing in the middle of the walkway, and people push past the two of us. "Hmm. OK. Why?"

"I don't want to tell you."

"OK, then."

I keep flipping. He hasn't labeled any of the flowers with their names, just with notes about where he found them. There's a white flower with scribbled handwriting that reads

"I found this one by that lake, you know the one, it was weird to go back" and another one that's orange and says "By my brother's new house, he seems really happy." Writing down where he found them is nice and all, but it doesn't help me much because I am looking for a specific type of flower, and clearly this guy knows nothing about the names of flowers.

"Have you ever been to the Scottish Highlands?" I ask him.

"When I was a kid," he tells me. He pulls me over toward a water fountain so that we're out of the way, and he leans against the wall, glancing up at the screen behind me to see if his flight has been delayed.

"Really?"

"Yeah. My family's from the UK."

"But you probably didn't collect flowers from there."

"No. That was definitely not something I did as a kid."

"Until you fell in love with your best friend?"

"Until I fell in love with my best friend."

Falling in love feels very weird when you are also grieving. I don't tell him that because I don't want him to ask who I'm grieving. I just think it, to myself. I feel my phone in my pocket buzz and I know it's probably Hanna, but I'm doing something very important and I know she'll understand. She's very understanding when she needs to be. Also very judgmental—two traits that don't usually go together, but somehow she makes it work.

"What exactly are you looking for?"

I put the journal down and look up at him. Instead of concerned, he looks curious now, which is a nice change of pace. I want people to be curious about me, not afraid for me. It probably helps that I'm not crying anymore and my eyes have cooled down to their normal color as opposed to the bloodshot red.

"Tansy. It's a flower. Or a weed if you want to call it that, but if you do call it that you're wrong, like I said. Also a rowan tree, but you probably couldn't press a tree in a book unless you just took like, a leaf."

He says, "Yeah, I don't know a thing about plant names. Not my area of expertise."

"It's not really mine, either, though I seem to know more than you do."

"You really care about plants."

"I kind of have to. My name is Laurel."

"And laurel is a…plant?"

"Mm-hmm."

It's nice to talk to somebody who doesn't know what a laurel bush is, because when I tell him it's a plant maybe he's imagining a beautiful flower and not a boring bush that's scattered everywhere across the country, long green leaves sprinkled across front yards everywhere. "It's very rare," I add, because I want to see if he will believe it. It's the opposite of rare, at least where I grew up, but he doesn't have to know that and I don't think he'll care much.

"Neat."

Neat is one of those words adults say to kids when they don't actually think something is very neat but don't want to overuse "cool" or "nice," so they just say neat. When he says it, it makes me feel like a kid, and I'm far from it.

I stop flipping through pages when I find a yellow flower that looks like it might be a tansy. It's hard to tell because it's pressed and all the pictures I've found of tansies are not pressed. I even google "pressed tansy flower" and nothing comes up, so I have nothing to compare it to. Next to the flower in the journal it says "Found this when I played in Toronto, it was on the side of the road and I made us all pull over so I could get it."

I take it out of the journal and say, "Can I have this?" I'm not normally rude, and it feels very rude when I say it, like it leaves a sour taste in my mouth.

He hesitates and then says, "Only if you tell me why you need it so badly that you followed me through security nearly twelve hours before your flight."

"My sister's name is Tansy."

"Yeah?"

"She's dead."

"Oh." He looks at me, really looks at me. Now there's that pity in his eyes, the sadness, like every time I bring up my dead family it injects everyone else with sadness. But with that, I see a bit of understanding in his eyes, too, which makes me feel worse because I don't want other people to understand, since that means other people have felt things like I've felt and that makes for a very sad world.

"My mom and my brother too," I add. Beside us, a woman glances up at me from the water fountain. I ignore her. I'm not sure why I'm telling him all this—maybe because I know that there's no way he'll say no to me taking the flower that might be a tansy now.

"Jesus." He shakes his head and then nods. "Take it."

I'm surprised because he doesn't say "I'm so sorry" or "I'm praying for you" or "What a terrible loss." He just tells me to take the flower and that's all. I pull it out of the journal, tell him "thank you," and then hand the journal back. "My dad is still alive," I add, because I don't want to be known as a girl with an entirely dead family, and I don't have to include the fact that he's at a glorified camp for sad adults. Then I turn around to walk away from the gates, or rather, practically run because seeing pity on people's faces makes me uncomfortable, and he has to catch a flight soon anyways. I wonder where he's going—I never did ask.

"I hope you get to kiss your best friend who you're in love with!" I call back to him. I don't turn around to see if he's gone red in the face, so I only imagine it instead. The idea makes me feel warm inside. I push past people until eventually I've disappeared from his line of sight and it's just me, the pressed flower, and hundreds of strangers in an airport in Kentucky.

I don't stop running until I find a gate where the passengers are going to Glasgow. The flight has been delayed twenty minutes and everyone there looks very tired. I know Glasgow is in Scotland and I wish I was going to Scotland. I know it's not a good idea, but I want to pretend right now. The chairs at this gate look squishy and relatively comfortable for airport chairs, which means they'll be good to sleep in anyways. Much better than the brittle waiting-room chairs at the hospital.

I take a seat and finally call Hanna. It doesn't even finish ringing once before she answers. Her "Hello?" is urgent and worried.

"I'm sorry I stopped talking to you," I say, talking over the worried questions she begins to rattle off. "But I found tansy."

"Wh...what?"

"Lowercase plant tansy, not uppercase person Tansy. The flower. It's a weird story but there was this boy with pressed flowers in a journal and he let me take one I think is a tansy. Can I send you a picture so you can look it up? I've tried but I can't tell for sure."

"You...oh my gosh, Laurel." Hanna sounds exasperated, but also kind of relieved, like a tired parent dealing with a small toddler who keeps running away.

"Sorry if I worried you."

"I'm—it's OK. But…please don't be mad at me." She hesitates, and I imagine her biting her lip and glancing around nervously like she always does. "I called your grandparents and told them you were thinking about running away to Scotland."

I almost laugh out loud because the idea sounds silly. I wouldn't be running away for good; I would just be looking for a tree and a weed. No, not a weed—a flower. The thought is almost funnier—imagine me going on an overseas flight just to find some plants.

"Your grandpa put a hold on the credit card he gave you."

"I have my own savings, anyways. I mean, I could still do it." Next to me, a man trying to sleep groans and pulls his hood over his head. It makes me want to slap him. Who expects to get good sleep in an airport anyways?

"You—you can't just run away from everything, Laurel."

"I'm not. I'm in Kentucky."

"Besides, I looked it up and most hostels in Europe require you to be eighteen years old. All hostels, actually. To be honest, I'm not quite sure if you could have checked into the hotel in Kentucky that your grandpa booked because you're underage and even if it was in his name, it would depend on how closely the desk attendant followed guidelines."

"Good to know."

"Yeah. But, I'm saying—you can't run away."

"It was just an idea," I say, though it felt like more than that—a miniature act of rebellion with only the thought of running. Something so incredibly un-Laurel that it felt monumental, even if it was just an idea and nothing more. "I've found tansy now, which will help my dad. And I have a plan to get something from a rowan tree without actually going to Scotland. Although I do wish I was one of those rich girls who travels to Europe every spring break with their family."

The man next to me puts headphones in his ears and leans away from me.

"Don't we all," Hanna says.

"Your mom designs houses for rich people, and your dad is a police officer."

"We've never been to Europe."

"True. But you could, if you wanted to. My family couldn't, especially not now."

"I get your point—what's your plan?"

The plan is still forming in my head, so I say, "It's a surprise." And then I tell Hanna I will text her, and I pretend I'm going to get some sleep here and then hang up the phone. I can tell she doesn't believe me, but she seems less worried when she says goodbye. There's still lightning outside, so all the planes have been grounded and the Glasgow flight has now been pushed back an hour. I wonder if the flower-journal boy is still sitting at his gate. I hope he won't be too late to wherever he needs to go.

My plan at the moment is to use one of the people at this gate to get the tree for me. Well, not the whole tree. I don't want to cut a tree down. That's bad for the environment and Mom always said trees had feelings. I just want a piece of the tree, like a leaf or a piece of bark.

The gate is very crowded, which means I have a lot of people to choose from. Most of them are sleeping or slumped over with their heads in their hands, and a few of the awake people just keep looking at the screen above the gate to see if it's been delayed even more. There's a little boy running around with his little sister, and his mom says to his dad, "I hope this tires them out, because this is a long flight." That makes me want to laugh and cry at the same time; it reminds me of my family and how utterly alone I am in this Kentucky airport. I wish Pumpkin was here—he would know how to cheer me up with a simple kiss on the face.

I set my sights on a girl who's typing furiously on a computer and looks like she's not much older than me. She has dark hair that nearly covers her eyes and there's a sticker for the University of Southern California on her laptop, so she's probably in college. I mostly pick her because of the aforementioned laptop, which tells me she can look up the image of a rowan tree. And if I really need to convince her, she can read the police report about what happened to my family and feel sorry enough for me that she'll help me out. I'm not afraid to pull the dead-family card if I have to. Not when it comes to this.

I approach her slowly and slide into the seat beside her. I'm sure the guy with the headphones is glad I've moved, as clearly my talking on the phone was wildly inconvenient to him. "Hello," I say. I'm getting very good at meeting people in airports. Although airports are where people seem to be the angriest, so perhaps it's not the best thing for me to do.

She doesn't respond because she has headphones in and is still typing furiously, so I tap her on the shoulder and wave. She jumps when she sees me, pulls the earbuds out of her ears, and asks, "What do you want?"

She's definitely an angry airport person, and I'm tempted to apologize and walk away, but then Ghost Rowan appears at my side and tells me to stop being so sensitive and suck it up.

"I need your help."

She motions toward the laptop. "I'm busy."

"Doing what?"

"Writing."

"Writing what?"

"Why do you ask so many questions? You sound like a three-year-old." She turns the computer screen away from me, so I can't see what she's been writing.

"I'm fifteen."

"Great. Good for you."

She's not as nice as the boy with the flower journal. I feel bad because I've clearly interrupted her very important writing, and she could be the world's next great author but because of me she's lost her train of thought and will never finish her novel. Ghost Rowan once again groans and tells me to stop being so dramatic.

She continues typing and I just sit there and stare until she finally sighs and says, "What do you need?"

"Are you going to Scotland?"

"Yes," she says flatly. I'm testing her patience. "I *am* at the gate for a flight to Glasgow, smartass."

"I need you to get something for me."

She frowns. "I don't even know you."

I reach my hand out to shake hers and say, "My name is Laurel. Now you know me."

"You're weird."

"I'm not going to Scotland but I need you to find me a tree that's in Scotland."

"Excuse me?"

"It's called a rowan tree, and then I need you to send me something from it, like a leaf or a branch. They probably won't let you send it overseas unless you press it and laminate it, like this." I hold up the maybe-tansy flower from the flower-journal boy.

"Why are you at this gate if you're not going to Scotland?" I wish she'd keep her voice down because I don't want the rest of the people at the gate to stare at us.

"Because I need something from the rowan tree. Obviously. And I know for sure they grow in Scotland. The Scottish Highlands," I tell her, remembering what Hanna said about the trees.

"What—? Why do you—? Seriously?"

"It's for my brother. He's dead. His name was Rowan and I don't think rowan trees grow in the United States, at least not natively, but they grow in Europe. My best friend Hanna told me they grow in the Scottish Highlands and if you're going to Scotland, you can go to the highlands and get me a piece of this tree so I can show my dad."

She closes her laptop and says, "And I should do all this for you just because you have a dead brother? We've all got dead people."

If Hanna were here, she would call the girl insensitive, because her words cut through the air like a knife. That would be ironic though, because sometimes Hanna is insensitive.

"They just died."

"They?"

"Yes. My mom and my sister too."

"That sucks." She sounds like she actually means it, not like she's just pitying me. Another flash of lightning strikes and the airport walls light up for a second.

"Why are you going to Scotland?" I ask her.

"Studying abroad," she tells me. Then she reaches into her bag and pulls out a tiny piece of paper. "Here. Write down your address. I'll try and find your tree but no promises, OK?"

"But you said you don't know me and everyone has dead people."

"Yeah, that doesn't mean I'm not willing to do it."

"You're weird."

"You too."

I write the address down and watch as she slips it into her carry-on bag. "Please don't lose it," I say, trying to keep my voice from sounding too desperate.

She snorts and says she loses almost everything so there's no guarantee, but she'll try her best not to lose this slip of paper with my address. "Must be important. If it wasn't important, you wouldn't have walked up to a total stranger at the gate for a flight that's not yours and interrupted my writing."

"Sorry about that."

"I was on a roll."

"Sorry."

She laughs, shakes her head, and then cranes her neck to look at the departure time on the screen. It's been pushed back another twenty minutes. The wind blows the rain against the giant airport windows. She asks, "Is your flight delayed too?"

To be honest, I'm not sure if it is, but I tell her yes because I don't want to have to explain that I'm at the airport eleven hours early and my flight technically isn't until tomorrow. She sighs, leans back, and says, "It's gonna be a long day." Then she puts her headphones back in her ears and closes her eyes. Once I'm sure she's not going to open them again, I peek into the pocket in her suitcase to make sure my address hasn't already gone missing. It's still there, so I cross my fingers that she'll remember. I peek into my own bag for the maybe-tansy flower, and then I decide it's probably a good time to get some overpriced airport food for myself.

I grab my things and disappear.

16

Mom ran away once. Dad and Mom used to joke about the story when we were growing up. My parents met when they were in high school and they were both supposed to go to the same college, but Mom decided she didn't want to go to college, and she booked a plane ticket. She was eighteen, and she called Dad from the airport and told him, "I'm going to Peru," and Dad said, "What?!" and Mom went to Peru for two months.

They never broke up during all of that. Mom didn't run away because Dad was tying her down, or because college was tying her down, or anything like that. She ran away because she wanted to, and then after two months she didn't want to anymore. Mom used to do most things just because she wanted to—she didn't need a rhyme or reason. When she came back, she wanted to go to school, so she got a degree in physics. Then she ran away from physics, because she didn't like it anymore, and got a degree in counseling instead. And then she ran away from counseling and made gardening her full-time job.

My mom's life sometimes sounds like a story in a book rather than an actual person's life, though I wouldn't call her a finicky person. She just liked to do what she wanted and said her soul would get heavy when she did things she hated.

She made it sound so simple. She would have never run away from Dad and me if it hadn't been for that truck.

My parents' love story is sweet without being loud. They met when they were young, and then all the running away happened and despite all the change, they were still in love. Even up until the accident, Mom would always kiss Dad on the cheek before she left to go shopping and he would always call, "Love you!" even when his nose was buried in a book.

They would joke about the Peru thing, like when Dad wouldn't answer his phone because it died and when he'd finally show up at home an hour late my mom would say, "Did you try and run away to Peru?" They'd both laugh, and eventually the rest of us would start joking about it too, like all the times when Rowan was out late at a party or Hanna, Lyssa, and I would miss the bus and have to walk home from school and would get home late. Hanna and Lyssa were even let in on the joke.

Running away to Peru right now sounds nice, but if I really did that, then I would have nobody to joke about it with. Ghost Mom grabs my arm and dances around, telling me to go to Peru, but Ghost Tansy and Ghost Rowan tell me I can't leave Dad alone. I want to yell at them because Dad left *me* alone, but I'm in the middle of an airport hearing ghosts, so it's probably best if I keep my mouth shut.

I'm not going to pull a Mom and run away to Peru. I do have people waiting for me at home who understand the joke. And besides, Hanna says I can't stay in a hostel until I'm eighteen, so when I turn eighteen, if I still want to run away—I will.

It's not fair, because Mom and Rowan and Tansy ran away for good, and it wasn't even on purpose. I wonder what they were doing when the truck hit. When we found them, we didn't know it was them, at first. We drove by and saw the ambulance and Dad said, "That looks bad." Then we saw that it was Mom's highlighter-blue car smashed into pieces and we saw a body on a stretcher and it felt like the world stopped in that moment—forever.

The lightning stops and planes start taking off again. I think about the laptop girl going to Glasgow, Scotland, and the flower-journal boy going to see his best friend who he's in love with. I imagine them slowly filing onto their planes, jamming bags into overhead bins, and finally finding their seats. It's comforting—in an odd way—to think of them taking their separate paths. The world keeps moving even when everything feels like it should stop.

I wish I'd asked the flower-journal boy for more advice, because being in love with your best friend is really an oddly specific conundrum and he seemed to know a lot about it. The fact that I've met somebody in an airport who had flowers falling out of his journal and who was also in love with his best friend makes me wonder if it really is that odd, or if maybe it happens all the time to people everywhere and we just put up with it until, eventually, we fall in love with a best friend who's in love with us too.

Hours pass as I drift in and out of sleep, sitting in a surprisingly comfortable chair in a random airport seating area with the pressed maybe-tansy held in between my fingers. It's not until three hours before my flight that they announce my gate, and of course it's on the other end of the airport. Luckily the Kentucky airport isn't nearly as big as the SeaTac one I'm used to, so the other end of the airport feels like a short stroll in comparison. I grab breakfast and settle in, watching as they put my flight information on the screen by the gate and people fill up the seats around me, all going to the same destination—whether it's home or just another somewhere else.

I decide to call Grandpa before the plane takes off. I've gotten nonstop calls from "HOME" since Hanna told my grandparents I wanted to run away. I didn't answer because

I didn't want to talk and also because sadness overwhelmed me every time "HOME" popped up on my phone screen. Before the accident, that meant Mom or Dad was calling me, and now it just makes me think about how both my parents are gone. One permanently, another temporarily—at least, I hope temporarily.

"Grandpa," I say into my phone, which is now nearly dead as I haven't charged it since the night before.

"Laurel." He sounds relieved. "We were worried."

"I told Hanna to tell you I'm OK."

"We were still worried."

"I'm calling to let you know I'm at my gate. I'm going to get on my flight soon."

"Your flight home?" he sounds scared when he says it, like he's afraid I'll change my mind again and decide to run away.

"Yes, Grandpa."

"We'll pick you up in a few hours then."

"But you don't like to drive to the airport."

"I'll manage."

In the background, Hanna's voice calls out "My mom can drive all of us!" and Grandpa laughs and says, "Oh yeah, Hanna's here too. And Lyssa."

"Tell them hi."

Grandpa lowers his voice and says, "I asked them to come over. Your grandmother was going bananas worrying herself to death about you, even though Hanna called and swore you were coming home. I asked them to come over to convince her. Hanna had to show her all your texts."

My heart drops a centimeter when he says "worrying herself to death," but then I recover so quickly it's as if death wasn't even mentioned. I'm getting good at recovering quickly. It's like one second I feel the ground pulled out from underneath me, and the next second I'm standing upright again, forced to move forward whether I'm ready or not.

"Well then, we'll all be there at the airport in a few hours," Grandpa continues.

"You act like I've been gone for months. It's only been a day."

"Sometimes you need people to act like you've been gone for months when you've only been gone for a day."

I'm not sure what he means by that, so I just say, "See you soon, Grandpa," and then I hang up and close my eyes. Soon they start to call off boarding groups and people form a line that stretches across the entire waiting area—most of them impatiently tapping their feet as they slowly scan boarding passes and move inch by inch closer to the gate. I'm one of the last people on the plane, even though I've been at the airport for nearly twelve hours. I'm not in a rush.

I score the window seat this time because I'm all by myself, which means hopefully I'll be able to catch some sleep. There's an old lady next to me who smiles and offers me a piece of gum, which I gladly chew as the engines rumble underneath us and we start to move.

Thirty minutes later, the plane takes off and I feel myself flying farther and farther away from Dad and Charles Sanctuary for the Recently Bereaved. Panic sets in when I think about it for too long. I imagine myself running down the aisle and pushing all the flight attendants out of the way, demanding to turn the flight around, then bursting through the door and jumping to the ground, running all the way to hug Dad. I take him home and make him promise he'll never leave me and I'll never leave him. But my life isn't a movie and my life isn't like Mom's life either. Instead, I sit in my seat inside the stuffy airplane with my head against the window and eventually fall asleep, and I don't wake up until we're less than an hour away from landing.

I feel dazed and confused because that's how it feels after you wake up from sleeping on an airplane, parched and hungry and stiff-necked. I sit there like a groggy zombie until the plane bumps against the ground and the wind rushes against the wings so loudly my ears pop. Next to me, the old lady grins. "That went by fast!"

I nod and try my best to smile back. I grab my backpack and hold it against my chest and laugh to myself, because for a moment I'd thought about running away with just this backpack, which only has one outfit in it. I want to call Dad and tell him I thought about running away because then we could make a joke about Peru, but I can't because he isn't allowed to have his cell phone at Charles Sanctuary for the Recently Bereaved. Also, I'm afraid the Peru joke is one of those things that probably died with Mom—just like the way she used to insist on buying records and dancing around to them in the kitchen, or the way she used to always slice her finger when she cut open avocados, or the way our flower garden used to be the most beautiful in the neighborhood and now it looks overgrown and thirsty at the same time.

When I get to baggage claim I'm immediately engulfed by hugs before I can even properly look at people's faces. Grandma and Grandpa and Hanna and Lyssa are all there to wrap their arms around me. Lyssa reaches me first and jumps onto my back, forcing me to give her a piggyback ride. Hanna buries her head in my neck, and then Grandma and Grandpa are at either side of me and they all hold on to me like they haven't seen me in years. The smell of Grandma's rose-scented lotion fills my nose as she pulls me against her skin. Tears fall down my cheeks and I begin to understand what Grandpa meant when he said sometimes you need people to act like you've been gone for months when you've only been gone for a day. Especially when during the course of that day you dropped your dad off at a mental institution across the country, and you chased a boy with flowers falling out of his journal, and you missed your dead family, and you seriously considered booking a flight to Scotland or Peru.

When I get home, I notice the subtle changes. I was only in Kentucky for two days, but it's like all the little changes that have happened between now and the accident are thrown into my face the minute I walk through the door. The way Grandma folds the towels—in perfect squares, whereas Mom preferred rectangles. And the way Grandpa scrubs down the kitchen counter so it's spotless, while Mom and Dad never cared much about that. The way the flowers in the garden are starting to wilt. The emptiness of the entrance to the house, which always used to be littered with Rowan's strewn-about jackets and Tansy's crayons that always seemed to roll across the house into all the nooks and crannies. Now it's clean. Too clean—as if it hasn't really been lived in. I guess it hasn't, not since the accident, because I wouldn't call what Dad and I have been doing living.

Since I've arrived home, Grandma won't stop pestering me to watch a movie with her. She's doing the thing where people say they just want to spend time with you but you know it's really because they're worried about you and they want to keep an eye on you. I don't really feel like watching a movie though, because I'm afraid one of the characters will remind me of Mom or Rowan or Tansy, like how Phoebe from *Friends* reminds Dad of Mom.

Grandma looks very tired though, which makes me wonder if I should be keeping an eye on her too. I suggest we watch a baseball game, because there's no way a baseball game could remind me of any of my missing people.

Dad always preferred books to sports, and Mom was one of those people who tried really hard to like sports when Rowan started playing soccer and I started playing volleyball, but she still clearly didn't understand. Tansy was the one who wanted to dance instead of play a sport with a ball, which made Mom say, "Thank goodness, I don't think my brain could have handled watching another ball be kicked or hit around." That made Rowan mad because he was very good at soccer and that was his *thing*—it was what he was known for. I was never that good at volleyball, and I don't think I ever will be because I'm not the right height to be anything but a setter and my hands always turn too far out when I try to set. Rowan made fun of me for that. It made me want to quit, but at the same time, he made me afraid to quit because he told all his friends I was going to be on the varsity team by the time I was a junior. Now I'll just have to quit, because not only am I not all that good, but it's become another thing that reminds me of Rowan.

Grandma leaves the room in the middle of the game. It sounds like she's crying, but I'm not sure why a baseball game would make her cry. Maybe it's because she wasn't paying attention to the game.

Grandpa pats me on the shoulder and says, "Glad to have you back here."

"When will Dad be back?"

He slumps his shoulders and says, "A few weeks? A month?"

"When will we get to talk to him?"

"Whenever he calls."

I play with the laminated maybe-tansy in my hands. Grandpa hasn't asked me about it, and I've been hiding it underneath my leg when Grandma comes into the room because if I tell her the whole story, we'll both end up crying. For now, it's mine. Although I really do need to go to a botanist to ask somebody if it's actually a tansy. I'm also kind of afraid to get an answer to that.

Dad doesn't call until the next morning. He says they get to use the phone at certain times during the day and that makes it sound like a camp for eleven-year-olds, not grown adults who are missing people. Either that or a prison. He asks me how my flight was and I tell him it was fine and leave out all the thoughts I had about running away. He says, "I miss you, Laurel."

"Is it helping you?" I ask him, "Staying there?"

"It's too soon to tell."

I lower my voice so Grandma and Grandpa can't hear me. "Don't kill yourself, OK?"

I can hear Dad's heart shatter over the phone. He says, "OK, Laurel."

"Promise."

"I promise."

"You can't leave me alone."

"I know."

"But you tried to."

"I know."

"Twice."

"Laurel..."

"Get better." I say it like a command, like if my voice is loud enough and strong enough it will happen. I'm going to will his recovery into existence—he has no other choice but to get better and come home to me.

I hand the phone back to Grandpa before Dad has a chance to say anything else. Grandpa and Dad exchange their I-love-yous, and Grandma gets on to tell Dad that he needs to make sure he's eating enough, then asks him about his roommate, about what kind of programs they have there, and about how the healing is going. Grandma talks about the healing process like it's equivalent to healing from a cut or a bruise. I imagine myself grabbing her by the shoulders and saying, "I can't just stick a Band-Aid and some ointment on myself! That won't bring Mom back! Or Rowan or Tansy!"

I don't say that, because I'm pretty sure Grandma talks about it that way because if she lets herself see how much worse than a cut or a bruise this is, she'll fall apart and never heal. It's easier to treat it like any other injury.

Mom always said I had an active imagination. I don't know how she knew though, because most of the things I imagine I keep in my head. She said it was because I was so quiet. "That means something wild must be going on in there." She'd tap my head and rub my shoulders and then continue on with her day. I miss her. I miss her like there's a bruise on my entire body that keeps getting worse and worse and doesn't stop throbbing. Ghost Mom puts her hands on my shoulders. Her touch makes the bruise sting.

Grandma hangs up the phone and goes back to making breakfast. Grandpa stands there for a moment and stares like he's still finishing up the conversation in his head. Then he goes into the kitchen, turns on the teakettle, and watches it heat up. I sit in my seat like a little kid waiting to be fed, and I watch them do very normal things under these very un-normal circumstances.

Though maybe this isn't un-normal anymore. Maybe this is normal now, because I'm scared Dad will be gone forever or he'll come back so different he won't be Dad anymore. I'm not sure what would be worse. I look up Charles Sanctuary for the Recently Bereaved on my phone to see what kind of activities and groups they'll be doing, but Grandma sees me and tells me I need to take a break from all the sad things. The site isn't super helpful anyways. It talks about healing and group therapy and narrative art, but what I really want is to know how it's going to help Dad. I want to know what he's doing— if he cries every night like he did at home or if he looks at old pictures of the five of us or if he ever thinks about me, *just me,* and how I'm here at home without him or Mom or Tansy or Rowan.

I tell Grandma the site isn't helpful and she says, "Laurel, it's not like they're going to have a livestream of your father's daily activities."

Personally, I think a livestream would be a good idea. It would be helpful for all the daughters who are scared their dads are going to kill themselves. Maybe I should write Charles Sanctuary for the Recently Bereaved a letter with the suggestion.

"Take a break from it," Grandma says.

I wish it was that easy. I wish I could close out of my family in my mind like a tab on the internet. I tell Grandma, "OK," and slide my phone underneath my leg to hide it from myself. It sits right next to the pressed maybe-tansy, which makes me think about the flower-journal boy and the computer girl who is probably in Scotland by now. I hope she finds a rowan tree and remembers to send me a leaf or a twig or really just a part of it. I'll even take the dirt it grows from. I just need to show Dad I found what he was looking for.

In the morning I call Hanna and ask her if we can go to a botanist. I really want to know if the tansy is a tansy, so I figure that's the best place to go to get answers.

"We'll want to go to a florist, actually," she says in her matter-of-fact tone. "Those are the people that own flower shops."

"I didn't know there was a difference."

"I looked it up."

Within twenty minutes of our conversation, Hanna and I are hopping on an almost-empty bus. We sit side by side in a row near the front, our shoulders bouncing off one another as the bus goes over bumps in the road and speeds up onto the highway to take us into the city. "It's not a long ride," Hanna says. "Only four stops." She's been looking at her phone the whole time, watching the map update our course to the botanist. I mean—florist.

I look at Hanna and think about how I want to hold her hand and how I also want to curl up in a ball and never leave my house again all at the same time. My feelings are very contradictory and jumbled.

The shop Hanna is taking me to is called Franklin's Floral. It's small, she says, but they have decent reviews online and it was the closest to our neighborhood. We walk across cracked sidewalks and eventually find the little shop with its bright pink sign and colorful flowers in the window. We step inside and somehow it's warmer—instead of the usual rush of air-conditioning in shops in the summer, we feel the heat intensify. Hanna grimaces and wipes her brow. A woman greets us with a cheerful "Welcome in!" and beside her, a boy stands behind a counter playing on his phone.

"We have a question," Hanna says. She doesn't even bother to browse or pretend like we're going to buy something. She's very straight-to-the-point about things. I sort of wish we were browsing, because there are walls full of bright green succulents Mom would have loved to put along our windowsill.

"How can I help you?" the woman asks.

"My friend has a flower." Hanna motions for me to pull the pressed maybe-tansy out of the depths of my pocket. "And we need somebody to tell us what they think it is."

"I think it's a tansy," I add as I hand it over to her. She turns it over in her hand for a minute with a frown on her face.

"That's a weed, not a flower," she says.

"I say it's a flower."

She purses her lips and then tells us to follow her over to the counter where the bored-looking boy scrolls through something on his phone. We follow closely behind, and I try my best not to get distracted by all the potted flowers by the desk. The lady clears her throat and the boy looks up and says, "Yes?" He doesn't look like the type of person who should be working in a flower shop. The shop has all these plants and bright colors and garden decorations and he's wearing all black and looks like he hasn't slept in days. It's funny in an ironic way. Hanna and I exchange glances and we both have to bite our tongues to stop from laughing.

"These girls are looking to get this flower identified. They think it's a tansy."

"A tansy is a weed," the boy responds. He doesn't even look up from his phone. I imagine myself grabbing his shoulders and telling him that a tansy is actually the name of my sister and my sister was a flower herself, so he better watch his tone.

"Well, they need you to identify it."

The boy sighs and then opens a drawer to take out a pair of glasses to slide onto his face. They don't look like they belong on his face, just like how he doesn't look like he belongs in a flower shop; they're much too big and they have purple rims, which makes me want to laugh.

The lady turns to us and says, "He's an expert. Knows everything about plants and trees and weeds and flowers. Even more than me, and I own the place."

"If you own the place, then who's Franklin?" Hanna asks. Hanna's always asking nosy questions.

"My brother," she says.

"Oh."

The boy holds the pressed maybe-tansy and turns it over in his hands. "Should have brought this in before pressing and laminating it," he tells me. He still doesn't look at me, as if he's talking to the maybe-tansy and not to a person.

"I didn't have it before then."

He runs his finger along the bumps of the flower stem and holds the yellow up close to his eyes. Finally, he speaks. "People don't press tansies often. It's not a particularly popular weed."

"It's a flower."

"Sure, kid."

"I'm fifteen."

"You're a kid."

Sometimes I really hate being fifteen.

He hands me the flower and finally looks up at Hanna and me with his sunken, tired eyes. "I'd say it's not a tansy—probably just another yellow weed. Could be a tansy, but there aren't many leaves and the stem is a little too thick, which makes me guess that it's not. If you wanted to know for sure you should have brought it in before you pressed it, and before it was totally dead."

"I didn't have it before it was pressed," I tell him for the second time. He ignores me and removes his glasses from his face, stuffing them into the drawer beneath the cash register.

"Are you looking for a particular flower?" the woman asks. "We can help you find it."

The boy adds, "Tansies grow all over here. Mostly in the mountains. The state considers them a noxious weed. You could probably drive up north an hour or so and find a ton. Then you'd for sure have a tansy to press."

I turn to Hanna. "I thought they didn't grow here," I say. She shrugs, then I look back at the boy and add, "It's a flower. Not a weed."

Hanna says, "Well, technically, it's both."

And the boy says, "What do you know?"

"Do you know where we could find a rowan tree?" I ask him.

He shrugs and says, "I'm not big on trees. They're native to Europe and Asia, yeah? But you could probably just go to the Arboretum—the one in Seattle. Should be there. Not natively, but you know."

"I'm supposed to get one in the mail. I might bring it in."

"You can't get a tree in the mail."

"Not the whole tree, *obviously*." He looks at me like I'm crazy and at this point, I honestly don't blame him for that. "You're supposed to know about plants," I add.

"Too many people are into trees. I'm more of a shrub guy."

"You're weird."

"You're the one claiming you're going to get a tree in the mail."

Hanna grabs my arm before I can insult him further and calls, "Thanks for your help!" as we scurry toward the door, past potted plants and succulents I wish we had more time to look at.

The lady who owns the place follows after us and tells us to give them a call if we need anything, or if we want to bring another flower in. She apologizes for the boy being rude, saying, "He's always like this, but the kid is obsessed with plants. He tries to play it cool, but you know, it's his passion, I'm sure of it. He dropped out of college last year. I'm trying to encourage him to go back…he could have a future in research, he really could."

I don't know why she feels the need to explain him to us. I look back at him; he's already on his phone and has headphones in his ears, which I don't think is something he should be allowed to do on the job. I can't imagine him doing research in a lab.

Outside, the air feels much cooler on my skin, and we walk quickly down the block, away from the store. Hanna says something about the boy being a jerk and seeming misogynistic. "Misogynistic" is Hanna's favorite word as of late.

Hanna takes the pressed not-tansy from my hands and looks at it as we walk along the sidewalk to who knows where. "Could be a bookmark," she says, which is exactly the kind of thing Dad would say and also the same thing I thought when I saw it. That's what happens when you grow up surrounded by people who love books. "We can go find a tansy if you want. I can ask my mom to drive us up north like they said."

I feel attached to the not-tansy. It reminds me of the boy in the airport who fell in love with his best friend. The flower-store boy said it could still be a tansy, and I like the story behind it, so I really want it to be a tansy. I could probably lie to Dad. He teaches English literature, not botany. I tell Hanna I want to keep this one and she asks, "Tell me again how you found it?"

"It fell out of someone's journal in the airport."

"And you stole it?"

"He gave it to me. Well, this particular one didn't fall out of the journal. I don't remember what flower did. A daisy, I think? Yeah. But I followed after him and he let me look at his flowers and then he let me take the tansy."

Hanna doesn't correct me or tell me that it's not a tansy, because it still could be.

"Why was he pressing flowers?" she asks. We pass the bus stop. Neither of us has anywhere to be, and coming out here to spend a total of ten minutes in a flower store feels silly. We might as well make use of our two-dollar bus tickets. Hanna suggests ice cream once she realizes that I'm not going to answer the question.

We walk into a brightly colored ice cream shop that's nearly empty, despite the heat outside. Hanna pays for us—she says it's her treat. I'm tired of people paying for me because my family is dead, but I don't protest because who would protest free ice cream? I order strawberry mint chip and Hanna gets cookie dough.

We find seats in the back of the shop. I can tell Hanna wants to ask me something but doesn't know if it's a good idea, because she keeps opening her mouth and then closing it, licking her ice cream to pretend like she was never going to say anything. Eventually, she manages to talk.

"You never answered my question."

"Which one?"

"The flowers and your airport adventure. Tell me about it." A part of me doesn't want to tell her about my night in the airport because it feels like I became a different version of myself there as I was bouncing around to people and asking them to do silly things for me. But she's Hanna and I'm Laurel so of course I tell her.

"A girl studying abroad in Scotland is sending me part of a rowan tree. At least, she said she would."

"Really? Wow."

"And the boy who gave me this was pressing flowers for his best friend."

"That's sweet."

"For two years. His best friend that he's in love with. It's a love story."

Hanna bites her lip. She pretends like she's licking ice cream, but she doesn't have any ice cream to lick off of her lips. Instead she's biting her lip to ward off the sudden discomfort because I'm her best friend who's in love with her. She eats her ice cream in silence and the awkward silence grows so loud she eventually has to speak.

When we stand up to throw away our ice cream cups, she says, "Laurel, listen…" Just that simple word sends a pang of anxiety down my chest and makes the ice cream curdle in my stomach. When somebody starts a sentence with "listen," it means they're about to say something very serious and probably very hurtful. "I've been wanting to talk to you about—about, you know, but it's just…my mom, she would—she wouldn't…she's so religious and…"

Hanna doesn't finish her sentence. I know what she's trying to say, but she can't bring herself to even call what happened a kiss, though it was a kiss, and she was the one who kissed me. An angry monster starts growing inside of me because Hanna keeps acting like if she just skirts around what happened it will disappear.

"At least you have a mom," I tell her. The words come out before I can stop them. They feel like poison slipping through my teeth. I swear, they make my teeth sting like when you take a bite of ice cream and your whole mouth tingles because it's too cold.

Hanna gapes at me and her eyes water, which doesn't happen often. She stops walking like she's frozen mid-step. We're standing just outside of the ice cream shop.

I keep talking. "I don't think now is the best time to talk to me about how your mom won't let you love girls because at least you have a mom to let you do things and you're the one who always says that you only like following rules if you agree with them, so why can't you break this one?"

I'm crying now too, except my tears are angry tears and hers are broken tears—they sound like shattering glass when they drip down her cheeks. People look at us when they walk past but nobody says anything. People don't like to see sadness up close; they just like to glance at it as they pass on the sidewalk and then forget about it and go on with their day.

"I—I hope you realize I'm grieving them too, and my feelings are all jumbled, and I...I..."

"They're mine to grieve." The monster grows angrier. I'm mad at Hanna for taking my grief and making it her own. It's mine—all mine—that's how it should be. Besides, that's not what we were talking about. How come my dead family always wedges itself into conversations?

Hanna looks around nervously. She blinks back her tears and wipes them on the back of her hand. "I—I need to go home."

"Then go home." This is quite possibly the meanest I've ever been to Hanna. It comes so naturally it scares me.

Hanna hesitates a minute before turning around and quickly disappearing down the street. I'm still crying and people are still walking past me like I don't exist. A part of me wants to run after Hanna and kiss her and tell her she shouldn't listen to her mom because her mom isn't here. Another part of me never wants to speak to Hanna again. I stand there frozen, breaking into pieces outside of the ice cream shop. The part that hurts the most is that Mom and Tansy never knew I was in love with Hanna—that I was the type of person to fall in love with girls. I never got to tell them.

I told Rowan. When I was twelve I said, "I think I might like girls." Rowan laughed at me and told me I couldn't know for sure because I was only twelve. He said I wouldn't know for sure until I kissed a girl. That seemed unfair though, because he knew he was straight before he ever kissed a girl, and nobody questioned him. Afterward, Rowan told me it wasn't a big deal anyways. "Being gay is pretty common nowadays." But if it wasn't a big deal, he wouldn't tell me I had to kiss a girl to know for sure. If it wasn't a big deal, I wouldn't have to keep it a secret.

And now a girl kissed me first and my heart hurts and I don't know if she'll ever be able to love me the way I need to be loved and I don't have a mom to go home to and talk to. That's what hurts the most. Ghost Mom puts her hand on my shoulder, and I shrug it off because what good is a ghost compared to the warm, bubbly Mom who used to dance around her garden?

Maybe Hanna isn't the best friend who's meant to fall in love with me back. That makes me very sad. I remind myself how mean I was to her. Maybe she was going to say something back that would change everything, but now I don't know if she loves me the way I love her or if she ever will.

19

"You've been sitting around your house like a bruised vegetable."

"That is a very interesting comparison."

"It's true."

Lyssa is standing at my door. That's what she does: she just shows up when she knows something is going on. Hanna and I haven't talked since our fight, but Hanna probably told Lyssa about it. Hanna also probably left out the reason why we were fighting because Hanna doesn't like to talk about her feelings. Lyssa is smart though, so she probably has an idea.

I'm glad Lyssa is here because my afternoon thus far has consisted of watching television and hearing my grandparents take turns crying in the kitchen where they think I can't hear them. Lyssa is here to save me—my knight in shining armor.

She says I need to do something non-dead-family related. She's decided we will do all the things she can think of that make people feel better. I tell her, "Happy things aren't going to make me feel less sad."

"Yeah, but they can make you feel happy, and if you're going to be really sad at least you could be slightly happy too."

I never thought of it that way. It sounds like the sort of thing Mom would have said. Dad used to joke that out of all the people in the world, one of my two best friends was exactly like my mom. When Dad said that, Mom said, "And her other best friend is exactly like her father." I've never thought of Hanna as someone who was very much like Dad, because Hanna is loud and sometimes blunt and Dad is quiet and likes to watch things from his seat on the couch. But they do both read a lot, and they're both the type of people who look very calm while underneath their composed exterior there's a storm raging. Maybe that's what Mom saw in the two of them.

Lyssa is taking me to yoga. I've never been to yoga before, and Lyssa insists I have to try it because it's "grounding."

"Since when do you even go to yoga?" I ask her.

"Since a few months ago."

"Why?"

She turns red in the face. "Well, actually, my foster parents own the studio. They let me take classes for free. They're not in today though, so don't ask about meeting them."

Lyssa looks at the ground when she says the last part, so I think she might be lying about her foster parents not being there today. Mom always told me that looking at the ground was a telltale sign of lying, and Mom was a counselor so she knew a lot about the things people said and did. Lyssa has never introduced Hanna or me to any of her foster parents. She says she doesn't want us to get attached, which is a very sad way of looking at things.

The yoga room is small, hot, and stuffy. There aren't that many people in the room, luckily, because it's a Wednesday in the middle of the day. Lyssa lends me one of the studio mats and says we're supposed to pay for them but since her foster parents own the studio we're off the hook. There's a middle-aged woman teaching the class who has a French accent and tells us to lie down on our mats.

"Breathe," she says. The room feels so stuffy it makes me want to hold my breath, but I do as I'm told. There's soft music playing in the background that sounds like it might be from the soundtrack to a movie I've seen, but I can't remember what movie. "Feel the ground against your body. Feel it giving you support, always supporting you, always there for you."

But in reality, the ground can't be all that supportive because it allowed a truck to hit Mom and Rowan and Tansy. And the ground really hasn't done much for me in terms of supporting me, and this yoga lady with the soft voice doesn't know what she's talking about. I'm mad at the ground. It had one job—to support me—and I feel unsupported by this world. I want to yell at the ground and punch it, and the thought makes me almost laugh out loud. The yoga lady tells us we need to trust our bodies to take care of us and that's when I stand up and leave the room because no matter how much my body does or doesn't do to take care of me, it won't help me get Mom or Rowan or Tansy back. I'm really mad and I don't think breathing will do me any good and I'm not sure why Lyssa thought this would help me.

I leave the room and run into a short woman with curly red hair—red enough to belong to a proper member of my family like Mom and my siblings instead of a knock-off Summers like me. She asks me if I'm OK and I say of course I'm not, because the ground isn't supporting me. She doesn't look at me like I'm crazy. She leads me to a bench and gives me a towel to wipe off the sweat on my forehead that accumulated from approximately ten minutes of sitting in the hot room. Within about thirty seconds, Lyssa bursts through the door with our mats rolled up under her arm. "Oh," she says, looking at me and the woman.

The red-haired woman says, "You must be Laurel."

I glance at Lyssa. She shrugs and says, "This is my foster mom."

"Penny," says her foster mom. She pats me on the back and adds, "Sorry the ground hasn't been supporting you lately." She sounds sincere, like she actually believes me and doesn't think I'm crazy. Mom would have liked her.

"Can we go home?" I ask Lyssa.

She nods and we walk in silence all the way to my house. With every step I take, I imagine myself crushing the ground underneath my feet for letting the world be so unsupportive. Finally, Lyssa asks me, "Hey Laurel…I've been meaning to ask…what happened with Hanna?"

I hesitate, and then I decide to tell her everything because she's Lyssa and that's what we do. I tell her about the kiss, the pressed not-tansy, the boy at the flower shop who looked very unhappy, and the argument Hanna and I had outside an ice cream shop. Lyssa puts her arm around me, squeezes, and doesn't let go until I finish talking.

Once I'm done, she shakes her head and smiles a bit and says, "So. Is this you properly coming out?"

That makes me laugh. Lyssa always knows how to make people laugh after they've said really heavy things, and I guess I haven't properly told Lyssa that I like girls until now, although I think she always knew because she knew I was in love with Hanna. *Am* in love with Hanna. I'm not sure. Love feels too heavy right now, and I always thought it was supposed to feel light.

We get back to my house and head straight up to my room. We change into pajamas, even though it's the middle of the day, and Lyssa turns on the first Harry Potter movie. "These always make me feel better," she says. They make me think of Mom and how Mom would only let me read one book a year and how I still haven't read the last two books. She wanted me to be the same age as Harry during each book. It was silly, yet Mom said it was her own experiment to see how much I'd connect to the characters. The problem is that I already know what happens because *everyone* knows what happens, and now Mom is gone so I guess I can read the last two books, but it feels wrong—like I'm doing her a disservice. I don't tell Lyssa that it makes me think of Mom though, because she looks so happy when the music starts and she leans her head back and sings along.

I start crying when eleven-year-old Harry gets his Hogwarts letter, and I'm not sure why—maybe it's because I want something like that to happen to me right now. Lyssa hugs me and rocks me back and forth and tells me it's going to be OK eventually. I want to believe her, I really do.

"You're totally a Hufflepuff," Lyssa says, still holding me tight as we watch the Sorting Hat sit on top of Harry's head. "And I'm a Slytherin. Definitely a Slytherin."

Eventually, Lyssa rattles off enough commentary to stop me from crying, and I start laughing instead. She tells me behind-the-scenes facts about the movie, like how the boys who play Fred and George skipped school to audition for the parts or how Emma Watson used to memorize every line and would get caught whispering them to the boys. Lyssa doesn't stop the movie every time I start crying—she just waits for me to start laughing and forget about why I was crying in the first place. Sometimes you have to sit through things that hurt until you can smile at them, even if they still hurt.

When the movie ends Lyssa asks me if I still want to find a tansy flower and a rowan tree. I tell her about the laptop girl who said she would find the rowan tree for me. I also tell her how I'm not sure because I really like the pressed not-tansy because it reminds me of the boy who fell in love with his best friend who fell in love with him back. Lyssa purses her lips and says, "I have an idea." She spends a while on her phone after that, and then it lights up with a text and she grins wide.

"Hear me out," she says.

"Um…OK. I'm listening."

"What if you got a tattoo?"

"Huh?"

She sits up and opens Pinterest on her phone to show me tattoos of flowers. "You could get their flowers tattooed on your body. That would be super cool. And meaningful! Plus it would last forever, so then you wouldn't need to go and find the tree or the flower."

I mostly want to find the tree and the flower to show them to Dad. I don't tell her that. The tattoo idea is actually cool, except for one thing: "But…I'm not eighteen."

Lyssa smiles even wider. "I know somebody." She shows me her ankle, where there's a tiny pinprick heart tattoo. "How else do you think I got this?"

"I didn't know you had that."

"I got it a few months ago. Don't tell Hanna, she'll throw a fit."

"I wouldn't dare."

Sometimes it feels like Hanna is our babysitter.

"One of my old foster sisters does stick-and-poke tattoos. Her name is Clare. She's like, twenty-two and has her own place, so we wouldn't have to interact with my old foster parents and she wouldn't get us in trouble. She's really cool. She has like a billion piercings. She's the one who dyed my hair for the first time."

There's a lot I don't know about Lyssa's life. I'm starting to think Lyssa might be the most secretive out of all of us, which makes me wonder if Mom was secretive because Mom and Lyssa had a lot in common. Mom seemed like an open book with her pages scattered all over our house. Now they're gone—evaporated into thin air.

"It could be a really small one. It doesn't hurt! Well, not much. It actually hurt a lot on my ankle. But that's because it's one of the most sensitive places on a person's body, so that's my fault. You could do like, your arm or your shoulder. That probably wouldn't hurt as much."

"I don't know."

"Come on." She turns so she's facing me and puffs out her lip to do the puppy-dog face. "I mean, I won't force you. I don't want to force you. But like, your dad would probably be cool with it anyways and I swear, it's safe."

"My dad is in Kentucky."

"Obviously, but when he gets back, he'll be cool with it. He's a cool-with-it kind of dad."

Mom was more of the cool-with-it one and my dad was cool with whatever my mom was cool with. Now that my mom is gone, my dad has nothing to go off of.

My phone lights up with a text from Hanna. She says she's sorry things are messy and she wants to talk with me sometime soon. Her name makes me angry suddenly, which makes me turn my phone off and look up at Lyssa and say, "Sure."

"Wait, really? Seriously?"

"Why not?"

"That's the spirit!" She claps me on the back and does a mini victory dance around the room. "I'll see when Clare is free. You don't have anything going on, do you?"

"Besides sitting around like a—how did you put it? Bruised vegetable?"

"Exactly that!"

We laugh and she grabs my hands and says, "You're going to get a tattoo!"

"An illegal tattoo."

"Oh, Hanna would *so* lecture us."

"I know."

Lyssa frowns and says, "Don't just do this because you're mad at Hanna."

"I'm not mad at Hanna." It's the truth. I wish it wasn't because I want to be mad at her, but I feel more hurt and confused, and also I'm starting to forget what we were even fighting about. The last time Hanna and I fought, we were thirteen and it was because she told on Lyssa and me for cheating on a math test. She claimed that the teacher questioned her about it and she gave in, but I was so mad I didn't even care. After a few days of fighting, Mom sat me down and asked me what we were fighting about. I told her and she said, "Is this something you'll still be mad about in a year?"

I frowned and said, "Of course."

She told me, "I don't remember what I fought about with my friends in middle school and I don't even remember what we fought about in high school. The things you fight about with your friends when you're thirteen blow over. Don't let it weigh you down."

I stopped being mad at Hanna that day. I wonder if the things you fight about with your friends when you're fifteen blow over like the things you fight about with your friends when you're thirteen. This feels like something else though, because it involves a dead family and Hanna trying to steal my grief and a kiss. It's not like cheating on a test.

I know rationally she didn't steal my grief—that can't happen. She was really close with my family and I'm sure she misses them too, but I can still be mad, even though it's probably weighing me down more than it should. Rowan would chastise me for being too sensitive and Mom would roll her eyes and not say anything to stick up for me, because she always hated it when we fought. And Tansy would have giggled but given me a hug, and I still wouldn't know what to do with all of the feelings that are swimming around inside of me, threatening to burst out at any moment.

Lyssa leans her head on my shoulder. "Please don't fight for too much longer."

"No promises."

"You two are impossible." She shakes her head and changes the subject. "So, the tattoo?"

"The tattoo."

Lyssa squeals and high-fives me. "Look at us! Being rebellious teenagers!"

"Who would have guessed?"

We crumple together into a pile of laughter. I'm glad I have a friend like Lyssa.

Lyssa's ex–foster sister, Clare, has a cluttered apartment in the Central District with duct-taped posters and tapestries covering the walls, which appear so thin I'm afraid they'll collapse on us. When she sees me staring at the posters she says, "The wall color is yellow. I had to cover it up."

Yellow was Mom's favorite color, and I imagine if she was here she would tear all the posters off, smile at the yellow color, then pull Tansy in close and say, "Yellow, like your flower." Tansy would smile her big, toothy grin and then ask me to show her the one I found in the boy's journal.

Clare hugs Lyssa and they talk for a while as if I'm not there. Lyssa kicks her shoes off and flops down onto Clare's faded old couch while Clare proceeds to talk about her new business and college classes. They ask one another about their lives, and it makes me think about how little I know of Lyssa's foster families. She doesn't like to talk about them. I wonder how many other foster siblings she's had, how many she's still in touch with, how many would give her friend an illegal tattoo in a tiny Seattle apartment.

I stare up at the posters on the walls, looking for something I recognize. They're mostly obscure bands and artists, ones maybe Mom would have known because she was always into local art. She'd take us to festivals when we were young and buy expensive paintings because she wanted to "support the industry." Dad always rolled his eyes at her, but he was the one who offered to take her to the festivals in the first place.

I'm so engrossed in the posters that I jump when I see Clare holding a steaming cup of tea right in front of me with an expectant expression on her face. I take it—the cup is hot against my hands and not exactly my drink of choice in the summer heat, but I'm not going to be rude. She stares at me for a moment with unwavering eye contact, which frankly makes me a bit uncomfortable, and then she speaks. "So. You want a little outline, yeah?"

At first, I don't know what she's talking about, like I've forgotten why we're here in the first place. "I mean, I can't do much more," she continues, "so that's what you're going to get. I want to be a professional tattoo artist one day, but that isn't going to pay rent at the moment."

Right, I think to myself, *Lyssa somehow convinced me to come here to get a tattoo.*

Last night, Lyssa and I spent hours scrolling through pictures of flower tattoos on the internet and eventually picked out a couple of photos to use as examples. One is a silhouette of a rowan tree with berries hanging from it and the other is a couple of sprigs from a tansy flower. The whole way to Clare's apartment, Lyssa kept talking about how healing it was going to be for me. "Not physically healing, obviously," she said. "I mean, physically, it *will* heal. Eventually. But it's going to be *so* emotionally healing for you." I printed the pictures out very small, not much longer than my pinky, and now I pull them out of my pocket to show to Clare.

"Can't do much smaller than that," Clare tells me. Lyssa thinks I should do something bigger, but I refuse because I don't want it to hurt that much, and also I don't want it to be noticeable. When I go back to school, I'm already going to be the girl with the dead family. I don't need to draw more attention to myself.

"Where?" Clare asks, holding the printed paper in her hands.

I point to my side, right above my hip, where my shirt will cover the tattoo. Clare says, "That'll hurt for your first one." Lyssa shushes her. I can't think of a better place, because everywhere else will be visible and I don't want people to see it, so I pretend like Clare's comment doesn't scare me and I shrug. I've gotten good at pretending to be braver than I really am.

Clare takes me into her bedroom, which is even more cluttered than the living area, and asks me to take off my shirt so that she can see her "canvas." Lyssa follows us and sits on the edge of Clare's messy bed. Clare starts rubbing alcohol-soaked cotton balls on my side, just like doctors do when they're about to give you a shot.

Everything that Clare uses for tattooing is kept in a black coffin-shaped box that's sitting on her bed right next to Lyssa. "She's a proper goth," Lyssa says. That makes Clare scoff.

I wish Hanna was here because she would be able to tell me if stick-and-poke tattoos are actually safe. Lyssa was clearly fine after hers, but Hanna would be able to tell me everything about stick-and-poke tattoos, like why people started doing them and what kind of ink they use and how much it's going to hurt.

We wouldn't be here if Hanna was here though, because Hanna would never approve of me getting a technically illegal tattoo. Maybe I should call Hanna and tell her I'm sorry because I miss her, and I miss a lot of people right now, but most of them I can't call, and I *can* call Hanna. But I don't call her because I'm afraid she might break my heart and I'm still slightly angry with her for stealing my grief, even though it's an irrational kind of angry.

"I'm going to draw it on you first to make sure it's what you want." I feel the Sharpie press against my side. I close my eyes, even though it's just a Sharpie, and Lyssa makes fun of me.

"I swear, it's not that bad," Lyssa reassures.

"I do it to myself all the time," Clare adds. She's covered in tiny tattoos up and down her arms. Nothing big, just a lot of small symbols and words, all in black ink.

Lyssa's phone rings while Clare is drawing on my side. "It's Hanna," Lyssa says. She grimaces, and I shrug as she steps out of the room to answer. I feel bad for Lyssa because she's been going back and forth between Hanna and me for the last few days. Just yesterday, she begged me to at least text Hanna back. I told Lyssa not right now and that's that. I guess it's just what happens when you have two best friends—at one point or another, you're going to be in the middle. I've been in the middle of Hanna and Lyssa many times before, and now it's her turn to be in the middle of Hanna and me and our brand new fourth friend: my grief.

"Take a look."

Clare hands me a mirror and I stare at the tiny plant silhouettes on my side. A tansy and a rowan for Tansy and Rowan. I wonder if seeing it on myself, even though it's just a drawing and not permanent yet, should make me emotional. It doesn't though, because it's just a drawing and not really Rowan and Tansy. Ghost Rowan laughs at me. "I can't believe you're actually doing this," he says.

"I like it," I tell Clare.

"Awesome."

She waits until Lyssa comes back into the room to start poking me with the needle. Lyssa looks upset and I'm about to ask her what's wrong, but then Clare starts dragging the needle across my skin and there is a sharp pain with each poke as she deposits the ink, black and blotting. I let out a yelp and Lyssa's expression turns from upset to excited. "Oh my gosh," she says, "It's going to look so good."

It hurts like a shot but without the part where they squeeze the medicine into you and you can feel it filling up your veins. After a few minutes of poking, it starts to hurt less, like my body has gotten used to it. Each mark she makes appears slowly, and sweat beads on her forehead from the heat inside her tiny apartment. She has to stop halfway through when her hand cramps up, which is a momentary relief for me. Despite how small the design is, it takes much longer than I would have expected—if Hanna was here, she'd explain that it's because I have to sit through each little poke, and if I'd gone somewhere professional it wouldn't take nearly as long.

Lyssa records the whole thing on her phone so I can watch it afterward. Clare tells her to stop getting in the way, because she keeps moving in really close with the camera. "But I need to document it all from all angles!" she protests.

"Document it from back there."

When it's all over, my side is bloody, sore, and bandaged. I don't really get a chance to look at the whole thing because Clare wraps it up almost immediately and my side is lightly bleeding anyways. "Take this off once you get home," she instructs. "Should heal easily since it's small enough."

"Thank you."

"Anything for a friend of Lyssa's." Clare winks at me and walks us to the door, back through the cluttered living room, and past the bits of yellow wall that stick out behind the posters. I make a mental note of asking Lyssa more about Clare, because I don't know much about Lyssa's foster families and I'd like to learn who they are. She knows everything there is to know about my family. Or rather, was to know.

"Your dad will like it," Lyssa declares after we leave the tiny apartment and stand on the sidewalk outside the building. Lyssa links her arm in mine and we start to walk away. I have no clue where we're going, but she seems to have something in mind. Then again, Lyssa is just that kind of person— she always seems to know where she's going, even when she has no clue.

"My dad is afraid of needles." Which is true—he was always squeamish about getting his flu shot, even as a middle-aged man. Mom used to make fun of him for it but deep down, I think she found it endearing.

"He'll like the gesture. The man went missing for days in a forest because he was trying to find those exact plants even though they don't grow here. He'd think it was poetic. He's a literature professor, for crying out loud."

"He also went missing because he wanted to kill himself."

"Kind of weird, huh? How he was looking for something at the same time as not wanting to exist?"

"It doesn't seem that weird to me. Not anymore."

We continue walking around a corner and begin our ascent up a steep hill. I figure Lyssa must have somewhere in mind because otherwise, I don't know why she'd choose to walk up this giant hill without a good reason. We don't talk as we power upward, but when we reach the top, Lyssa finally asks: "Do you think he's getting better?"

The question sits in the air for a moment, the two of us slightly out of breath and standing still at the top of the hill. "You and Hanna need to stop asking me that."

"You haven't talked to Hanna in a week and this is the first time I'm asking you that question." She shakes her head and then continues walking. I have to jog slightly to catch up, my feet nearly tripping over cracks in the sidewalk.

"Sorry."

"It's OK. You can snap at me. Just don't expect me to sit there and take it like Hanna does."

I've never thought of myself as the type of person who snaps, and I've never thought of Hanna as the type of person who sits there and takes anything. But maybe that's what it looks like to Lyssa, and my version of everything is all skewed. Lyssa puts her arm around me and keeps talking. "I get it. I won't talk to you about Hanna anymore, or your dad, or your family. At least, not today. We'll keep today focused on the beautiful experience of your stick-and-poke tattoo. But you should see a therapist or something, OK?"

Lyssa goes to therapy every other week. She talks about it very openly, which is something I really respect about her. Hanna always says she wishes she could be as open as Lyssa. That makes me wonder what Hanna's hiding deep down.

I want to go home and talk to Dad on the phone, but he only calls us on Tuesdays, Thursdays, and Sundays. It's a Friday so he's not going to call for two more days. "Where are we going?" I ask Lyssa, surprised she hasn't told me by now.

"It's hot out," she declares. "I want to go swimming. There's a lake west of here, we could walk. Madrona—you ever been?"

I haven't been, and I protest at first—I would still rather curl up at home—but Lyssa convinces me because it's pushing ninety degrees outside and I'm sweating so much it looks like I've jumped into a lake anyways. "It's summer," she tells me, dragging me along behind her as we travel downhill toward the water. "I know it's like, a really messed-up summer for you, but you should at least do a few normal summer things. Like swimming! Besides, you can show off your tattoo."

"It's bandaged. And I don't have a swimsuit."

She waves her hand and shakes her head. "Whatever." She glances down at my side, lifting up my shirt and eyeing the bandage. "I'm so excited to see it all healed. I mean, they're on you forever now. Maybe I should get a tattoo for my mom."

"That would be cool."

I know Lyssa has a dead mom too, but it feels like she doesn't understand that, even without the tattoo, Tansy and Rowan and Mom will be latched onto me forever, and I don't know if it's a good or bad thing. Lyssa wants her mom to be latched onto her. Lyssa's told me before that her memory of her mom is fading and things feel really distant, so she wants to hold on to everything she can. But me? I just wish I could set it all down. It's too heavy and the tattoo didn't take any of the weight away.

The grass by the lake is littered with teens wearing brightly colored swimsuits and putting sunscreen on one another's backs. Any other summer, Lyssa, Hanna, and I would be just like them—probably gossiping about people at school, telling one another stories and dreams, letting the sun coax the freckles on my nose out of hiding. But this year, it feels as if I'm living on the edge. All the people at this lake are doing what I'm supposed to be doing, but I'm stuck in limbo now.

Lyssa can tell I'm thinking of my parents, because she grabs my hand before I have a chance to wallow in the sadness any longer and drags me toward the water. She tosses off her shirt so she's wearing only a sports bra. "My clothes will get all wet," I tell her.

She shrugs. "Who cares? It's summer."

Maybe I'll let myself pretend—just for a few minutes—that there's nothing to worry about because it's summer, and I'm fifteen going on sixteen, and everything is supposed to be light-hearted and easy. Except as Lyssa drags me to the dock and I slip off my shoes along the way, leaves crunch underneath my feet and I know without looking down that they're laurel leaves—a cruel reminder of Mom. Mom named me Laurel and now she's gone. Lyssa takes my hand and I close my eyes real tight.

"Three! Two! One!" she calls, and then we're jumping. The water is cold against my body, washing away all the sweat and grime from our journey here. Water goes up my nose and I squeeze my eyes closed, staying underneath for a bit longer than Lyssa, feeling my hair fly up all around me and the bubbles pass by my face. Maybe if I stay underwater long enough, it will feel like a proper summer.

But eventually I emerge from the water, deep breaths filling my lungs, because it's not a proper summer—it's so far from it.

21

Ghost Mom visits me at night. Apparently, she likes to show up and have important conversations in the middle of the night. That's what she was like when she was Alive Mom too. She would knock on my door right before I turned my light out, sit on the foot of my bed, and ask me about my day. I would say, "Mom, I'm tired," and she'd say, "Laurel, you didn't talk much during dinner and I want to know how your day was." So I would tell her, and then she would tell me about hers, and sometimes she'd talk about the stars and why they're probably the root cause of all my problems.

She's much more vivid this time. Instead of just feeling and hearing her, I can see her too. She's wearing a bright yellow dress, the one she said was the same color as Tansy's flower; her red hair is shining like it did in the sun, even though it's the middle of the night in my dark room. She sits on my bed and lifts up my shirt to see the rowan and tansy on my skin.

"A beautiful experience," she whispers. Her voice sounds like an echo.

"That's what Lyssa called it."

"Oh, of course she did."

"What are you doing here?"

Lyssa told me ghosts only show up when they need something from you, and I want to know what Mom needs from me. Ghost Mom doesn't answer my question. In the corner of my eye, I can see my phone buzzing with texts from Hanna asking me to reply to her, and the streetlight outside of my house keeps flickering. The brightness of my phone screen and the flashing lights and Ghost Mom's red hair all make my eyes hurt. Ghost Mom wraps her arms around me to hold me still. I'm not sure how a ghost manages to hold on to an alive person, but it works.

"I miss you," I whisper.

"I'm right here."

"But you're not."

She doesn't have an answer for that, either. The silence makes me start crying, and she asks me to talk to her, so I tell her about everything that's happened since she left—about Dad going to Charles Sanctuary for the Recently Bereaved, and how I only get to talk to him on the phone three times a week, and how Hanna and I are fighting, and how Hanna and I kissed, and how my tattoo hurts because the skin is scabbing over, and I really want to scratch it but I know I'm not supposed to.

"Oh, Laurel," Ghost Mom says. "My sweet, sweet Laurel."

"I'm not sweet."

"You are."

"I kept secrets, and I wish I hadn't."

"Everyone keeps secrets."

"But I should have told you."

"Told me what?"

I swallow hard. "A lot of things. I should have told you about Hanna and I should have asked you for advice because I don't know who to ask now and I miss you barging into my room at night and practically forcing me to tell you about my day. I never told you everything about my days and I wish I had."

I'm reminded of the night Hanna kissed me. That night, I was quieter than usual, though Dad and Rowan and Tansy didn't notice because I'm always quiet. Mom noticed. She sat in bed with me and asked me if I was upset and I said, "I don't know. Something happened."

"What?" she asked. I never told her. I just started crying and then she rubbed my head until I fell asleep.

Ghost Mom says, "You're telling me now."

"But you're a ghost, and it's all my fault because I wanted pizza instead of ice cream."

"Oh, Laurel. Please don't hurt so much. You have all the time in the world."

Mom, Rowan, and Tansy all wanted ice cream. "Let's skip dinner tonight," Mom said, but I wanted pizza. I was too hungry, so I made Dad take me and we said we'd meet up with them afterward. Except we didn't—not in the way we wanted to. Instead we drove by their car all smashed up and then we met them at the morgue. We never made it to the ice cream shop or the pizza place.

"I have all the time in the world for what?" I ask. Ghost Mom doesn't have the right to tell me not to hurt so much because she's the one who left me behind, and if it had been the other way around, she would be hurting this much and I wouldn't tell her not to; I would understand that she couldn't control it.

"For love, for everything. You're only fifteen."

I don't see Ghost Rowan, but he says, "You don't even know what love is yet."

To which Ghost Mom says, "Quite the opposite. People learn what love is when they're toddlers. And when they're fifteen? It hurts so much it feels like the world might fall apart. But you have time to figure out how to love."

Ghost Tansy sighs, "Aww."

Their voices are like a chorus in my brain that keeps getting louder and bounces off the walls of my head, and I can't lower the volume no matter how hard I try. My tattoo hurts, but Ghost Mom's arms are wrapped around me so tightly that I can't move to make it hurt less.

"Tansy didn't get time," I say. My voice grows louder and I'm yelling now, and I don't care if I wake up Grandma or Grandpa. "Rowan didn't get time! You didn't even get enough time! Why do I have all the time in the world?!"

Ghost Mom tells me I can't live my life like I'm running out of time. She tries to pat my head like she used to every night, but I flail away from her. Then suddenly she's everywhere. I can't get away.

"Shut up!" I scream at her to stop talking, but she keeps saying the same thing in her singsong voice that used to be so comforting for me but is now just haunting. "Shut up, shut up, SHUT UP!" She doesn't stop.

It never stops.

22

I wake up in the hospital.

Yes, it's because the tattoo got infected. Yes, because I wasn't supposed to jump into a dirty lake right after getting an illegal tattoo. How was I supposed to know? Clare didn't tell me, and Lyssa is reckless like that. She's gotten a tattoo before, so I assumed she'd tell me if I was doing something really bad. I've already been told it was a stupid thing to do about seventy-five times by my grandmother. "A *tattoo?*" she says, as if it's the equivalent of cutting off a limb. "Laurel? A *tattoo?* Seriously?"

She's upset, though I think she's more upset about the fact that I got a tattoo than the fact that it got infected and gave me a fever so high that I started hallucinating about Ghost Mom. Apparently, I had such a high fever that I sweat through all my sheets and Grandpa had to drive me to the ER in the middle of the night. Oops.

I'm just glad the doctors don't ask a lot of questions about how I got the tattoo in the first place, because I don't want Clare to get in trouble for giving me an illegal tattoo.

This is the fourth time I've been to the hospital in the last few months. I feel pretty stupid, but at least I'm not in the psych ward so I won't have to see the apologetic nurse. I don't want him to feel even more sorry for me, because at this point, the number of bad things happening to me is just embarrassing.

The doctors give me some big blue pills to make the infection go away. They had to cut off some of my skin, and now the Rowan tree is missing its bunch of berries. The whole tattoo looks more like a smudge now. They're having me stay here a few more hours until my fever breaks, which is probably more for Grandma's sake, since she got really worked up about it. She freaked Lyssa out pretty badly—once she saw the infected tattoo, she knew Lyssa was somehow involved and immediately called and forced her to meet us at the hospital. Even though I was really feverish, I swear I could hear her yelling at Lyssa in the hallway.

"Your father is going to be so upset," Grandma says after the doctors leave me alone with my grandparents. I feel pretty fine, just a little sweaty, and my side hurts from where they made the incision.

"I thought he would like them," I say.

"It doesn't matter if he would like them, Laurel! It's a tattoo! And you're fifteen! What has gotten into you?"

Grandpa sets his hand on her shoulder. She sucks in her breath after she says that, because it's pretty obvious what's gotten into me: my mom and brother and sister died all because I wanted pizza.

I look down at the smudge of a tattoo on my side. "It was a tansy," I mutter. "A tansy and a rowan tree. Except now it's just a smudge."

The anger falls off of Grandma's face and is immediately replaced with sadness. She crouches down next to me and places a hand on my cheek. "My beautiful, sweet girl. You made a stupid decision, but you are my beautiful, sweet Laurel Summers." She drops her head down to my shoulder and whispers, "I was scared we would lose you too, Laurel."

"It was just an infection."

"We didn't know that. You were yelling at the air and sweating up a storm."

"I'm sorry."

"Oh, don't be." She kisses me on the cheek and then releases me and wipes her eyes. "I just overreacted."

Grandma is one of those people who can change moods in the blink of an eye. She can be really mad and then, suddenly, she's kissing me on the cheek and patting my hand. When I was little, I asked her about it, and she told me, "Sometimes emotions aren't worth holding on to for too long." Still, Dad used to tell us that it was a terrifying thing to grow up with. Mom always loved Grandma Lucy; she said Grandma Lucy was the best mother-in-law she could have ever asked for.

"Don't tell Dad about this. Please." The thought of Dad getting a call at Charles Sanctuary for the Recently Bereaved about his only remaining child being sent to the hospital makes me shiver. He would be so worried; I don't know what he'd do. He's already tried to kill himself twice, and both those times happened when he knew I was safe and sound. That almost makes it worse—I was perfectly healthy and present, but he still wanted to leave me.

"Oh, I wouldn't dare," Grandma says, "You're going to explain this all to him when he comes home and sees you have a tattoo."

"I bet you he'll like it."

"I bet you he won't."

"I hope he comes home soon."

"Me too."

Grandma squeezes my shoulder and then moves aside so Grandpa can sit with me. He tries very hard to be stern, but Grandpa has never been all that good at being stern. He has a permanent smile in his eyes. One time, when we were kids, Rowan gave Tansy a haircut when we were visiting them, and Grandpa was the only one home. He tried so hard to lecture us but ended up laughing at how silly Tansy looked. It's a funny memory, besides the part where Grandma got home and found us.

"You should have told us about it at least," Grandpa says to me. "Then we would have had a clue as to what was going on. Thought you had some deathly fever."

"Sorry."

"Shush. I'm sorry."

"For what?"

He shakes his head and lifts up his arms. "All of this. Everything that's happened."

"Shh. That's on The List."

"The List?"

"The List of Things Not to Talk About with Laurel. Apologizing is one of them. I'm tired of people saying sorry to me."

Grandma shakes her head at me, but Grandpa laughs his deep, hearty laugh. It makes me smile, and for a moment I feel like Laurel again, the Laurel who makes silly jokes and hugs her friends and is very good at keeping quiet when she needs to and doesn't do disruptive things like getting a tattoo. That version of Laurel is slowly disappearing, but I feel like I'm her again right now, laughing with Grandpa.

Another voice breaks through our laughter. "I—I didn't throw The List away, you know," she says. Hanna stands in the doorway, slightly out of breath. She reaches into her pocket and pulls out a crumpled piece of paper and smiles at me shyly, like we've just met. "I have it here. If you want it."

"You told me it was a bad coping mechanism."

"That doesn't mean I threw it away." She bites her lip and then she adds, "I'm really sorry."

"ON THE LIST!"

At first, she looks like she's scared of me, but then I smile, and she smiles too. I say, "I'm sorry too. And it's not violating The List if *I* say it."

Hanna flies across the room and attacks me with a hug. "Ouch," I mutter. Hanna is known for having very strong (and rare) hugs, and the intensity is heightened by the fact that my tattoo was infected and stings when she bumps it.

"I'm sorry we weren't talking," she whispers.

"I'm sorry I was the one ignoring you. And I'm sorry for saying you stole my grief."

"I'm sorry for being so worked up about what my mom thinks, and I'm sorry I can't…I haven't been able to…"

"We can talk about that part later."

"I'm a terrible friend."

"You're my best friend. Things are jumbled."

"I think we violated The List a couple of times."

"You apologized first, so it's your fault. You started it."

"Oh, great." She rolls her eyes, which is a very classic Hanna thing to do, and then finally releases her grip on me. She sniffs and blinks to hold back tears. Hanna has been crying a lot lately, and Hanna is not a crier. Behind her, Grandma and Grandpa both move slowly toward the doorway, giving us some time alone.

"I suck at feelings." Hanna sniffs when they're out of earshot. "And I don't know if I'm ready to tell my mom and I don't know how I feel and everything is really…awful."

I remember what my fever-induced hallucination of Ghost Mom said about only being fifteen and having time for love and for all the feelings. I tell Hanna, "I don't know how many feelings a person can possibly have but I definitely have too many right now."

"I miss them," she whispers. "I miss them a lot."

"Me too."

"I love you."

"I love you too."

She holds my hand and squeezes. We're both crying now, and I'm not sure if it's because we miss my mom and my siblings, or because we're in love, or because we're not in love. Maybe it's all of the above. I wonder if you can be both in love and out of love at the same time, because that feels like where we are—this weird place of not knowing which one we are, or which one we should be.

I wish Mom was here to tell me what to do. Ghost Mom can only do so much. Plus, the Ghost Mom that gave me love advice was apparently a fever-induced hallucination, so I suppose I should take her advice with a grain of salt.

"So," Hanna finally speaks, "you got a *tattoo?*"

I cringe because I half expect her to lecture me about it, but instead she laughs and asks, "Can I see it?"

"It's more of a smudge now because it got infected." I turn so she can see my smudge tattoo.

"That's a tree, yeah?"

"Rowan tree. And a tansy flower, but they've kind of blended together into one."

"I love it," Hanna says.

"You won't love how I got it."

"Oh, I'm sure I won't."

I tell her about Clare, the ex–foster sister, and about how her apartment was dingy and covered in posters. I tell her about the stick-and-poke tattoo and how it hurt but not as much as I thought it would. I tell her about how we went swimming afterward and she says, "Oh my God. You're not supposed to do that." Hanna—the person who plans to never get a tattoo in her life—apparently knows more about tattoo aftercare than both Lyssa and me combined.

"I'm aware. Hence, the infection."

"You two are idiots."

"Also aware. Grandma Lucy made sure to let Lyssa know she thought so."

"Oh, poor Lyssa. Although, she kind of deserved it. But… poor Lyssa."

"Yeah!" Lyssa says, her voice traveling in from outside the room, "Poor Lyssa indeed!" Lyssa is standing in the doorway, still wearing her pajamas from when Grandma presumably woke her up in the middle of the night. "I heard my name and figured it was my cue to join the conversation."

"You're an idiot," Hanna tells her to her face.

"But I'm a cute idiot!"

"Debatable."

Lyssa tosses her sweatshirt at Hanna and nearly hits her in the face, just missing me. Hanna tosses it back and hits Lyssa right in the forehead. "Careful!" I call. "I'm injured!" They both snort and toss the sweatshirt over my head. I close my eyes underneath the soft material because if I can't see, then I don't have to be aware of the fact that I'm in the hospital and the circumstances of this whole day are incredibly absurd. Instead I can pretend that it's just like old times when Hanna, Lyssa, and I would play around in the backyard. Mom would point the hose at us from her garden and Dad would call us inside for dinner; Rowan would threaten to steal our food and Tansy would try and get us to play games with her. I miss it. I miss it so much I don't think there are any antibiotics in the world that could heal my heart.

"Can we take you to find the tansy flower?" Lyssa asks me softly. The sweatshirt is still over my head.

"I like my not-tansy flower." The little laminated, pressed flower is still in my pocket. It hasn't left my side for days. "But you can still take me, if you want," I add. I say it more for them than for me. Hanna slips her hand into mine and squeezes.

"It'll be fun," Lyssa says.

"Just like how you two getting tattoos was fun?"

Lyssa leans over me and hits Hanna in the shoulder. The three of us laugh and the sweatshirt falls off my face and gets tossed around the room until the doctor comes in and tells us to stop roughhousing. She takes one look at me and says, "Seems like your fever broke."

"Sure did."

"Let's get you checked out. Just promise us you won't go swimming after getting tattooed by an unlicensed tattoo artist again."

"Yes, ma'am."

23

Grandma and Grandpa make me start seeing a therapist and honestly, it's not the worst idea they've ever had. Hanna and Lyssa both think it's a good thing too, so I don't really have much of a choice. Mom was always saying everybody should go to therapy, but Mom never went to therapy herself, so it was kind of hypocritical.

My therapist is named Shannon. She has very short hair and a warm face and wears colorful dresses. She takes me into a room where I can sit anywhere I'd like, and she leans in to-ward me when she talks. She reminds me of Mom and how Mom spent a year counseling people and two years before that getting a degree to do so. Yet she hated it, which makes me sad. I hope Shannon doesn't hate it like Mom did. It feels like something important to mention, so when she closes the door, I say, "My mom was a therapist and she hated it. So, if I make you hate it, I want you to tell me and I'll stop coming."

Shannon chuckles, which is not the response I was expecting, and says, "Don't worry. I've been doing this for years." She looks very young, so I'm not sure if she's been doing it for enough years, and I'm still worried I'll make her hate it. She says she has to ask me questions to assess me and we can buzz through them if I want, or we can spend a long time unpacking each answer. She asks me about my gender and sexuality and relationship status and doesn't even blink when I tell her I like girls. I kind of wish she did though, because I've never told an adult before and I want it to feel like coming out, not just going through a checklist.

We get through several more questions, and then she asks, "Do you live with your parents?"

I know Grandma and Grandpa made this appointment for me so they must have already told Shannon about my family situation, but she has to ask the question anyways. I swallow and I tell her my mom is dead and my dad is at Charles Sanctuary for the Recently Bereaved. She nods and doesn't gasp or say "I'm sorry," which is a nice change from the usual reaction. Maybe therapists have to be calm all the time—maybe that's part of their training. Maybe that's why Mom couldn't do it, because Mom was anything but calm— she was a raging storm all the time, but in a colorful, light kind of way.

"How have you been holding up with all of that?"

"Is that one of your checklist questions?"

She laughs. "No, it's not. I just wanted to ask, but we can move on to the next question if you would like."

"I would like." She nods and then looks down at a sheet of paper. Before she has a chance to ask me the next question, I interject, "But badly, for the record. Not as badly as my dad. I got a tattoo for them, though it got infected. Also, my dad left me in a laurel bush."

She raises her eyebrows and says, "Care to elaborate?"

"Not really. It's on The List."

"The List?"

"I made a list. Of all the things that I don't want to talk about. It's called 'The List of Things Not to Talk About with Laurel.' My best friend Hanna wrote it down, or at least, she wrote part of it down until she decided it wasn't a healthy coping mechanism."

"We should get a copy of that list."

"Hanna has it."

"What if we made our own version of it, right here? We've got plenty of markers and paper. I'll even close my eyes while you make it if you want me to. We're done with the intake assessment anyway."

I like Shannon because she offers to close her eyes while I make The List. I'm tired of people watching me like I'm a ticking bomb about to explode.

"Aren't you going to tell me it's an unhealthy coping mechanism?"

She shrugs. "Anything can be an unhealthy coping mechanism if you use it the wrong way."

"Like getting an illegal tattoo and getting it infected."

She laughs. "I suppose so."

"Next to that, making a list doesn't sound so bad."

"Do you want to write out your list for me?"

"Can I do it at home?"

"Sure. Bring it in next week so that we can talk about it."

"But we're not supposed to talk about the things on The List."

"Hmm. OK. How about we draw about it?"

"That seems like cheating."

"A loophole."

I don't want to draw the things on The List, but that sounds better than talking about it, so I agree that I'll make it at home and bring it in and *maybe* we will draw things that have to do with it, assuming she closes her eyes while I draw.

Shannon asks me more questions about my friends and my grandparents. I tell her about Hanna and Lyssa and some of the weird things the three of us have done together, like making music videos when we were twelve or painting our faces for Halloween. She tells me I don't have to talk about Mom or Dad or Tansy or Rowan unless I want to. I like that—everyone else keeps trying to make me talk about them, even Lyssa, who's supposed to get what it's like to have a dead family member.

"Does this time work for you next week?"

"I might be too busy moping around my house like a bruised vegetable." She shakes her head and I add, "That's what Lyssa called me the other day."

"Lyssa sounds like a character."

"She is. But yes, this time will work for me because it's summer and I'm not doing anything."

"Perfect. I'll see you then. And you'll bring your list?"

"Yes, ma'am."

"OK, Laurel. Take care. You can give us a call if you need anything over the next week."

"Thanks."

Grandpa picks me up. He doesn't ask me how it was because Grandpa isn't a big fan of talking about feelings. He smiles at me very big and I smile back. I think there's an unspoken acknowledgment that it went well and that I actually don't hate counseling. I still can't help but worry that Shannon might secretly hate counseling, just like Mom did. When I get home, I tell Grandma about that worry and Grandma says, "Your mother had a big heart. Sometimes too big."

"Is that a bad thing?"

"Not bad. Just…heavy. It weighed her down."

"My heart feels heavy."

"Mine too, Laurel. Mine too."

Dad calls in the evening. He doesn't sound like himself, but he sounds more like himself than he did a few weeks ago. I wonder if he'll ever really sound like himself again or if he'll become a new version of Dad, just like I'm becoming a new version of Laurel—the version that exists without Mom and Tansy and Rowan. I tell Dad that I started going to therapy and he sounds really happy about it. I leave out the part about the tattoo because that's something I'll wait to mention until he gets home—I don't want him to worry about me and how it got infected and how I ended up in the hospital. Grandma keeps nudging me and pointing at my side because she wants me to bring it up. I push her hands away and keep talking to Dad about everything that's not related to the stupid tattoo.

"I've met some really cool people here," Dad says, "Some really strong people. Their stories are…inspiring. Just inspiring. I've gotten so many ideas for my novel."

Dad's been writing a novel for about ten years. Rowan always said that it would never get finished, but Mom believed it would. Mom may have been the only person in the world who believed Dad would ever finish his book. Even the other professors at the university would joke about it. One time, Dad got an outstanding-educator award from the English faculty, and when this squat man with a bow tie gave a speech to introduce him, he included a joke about Dad and his novel that was never going to be finished. Rowan laughed really hard at that, and even Tansy giggled. Mom shook her head and whispered to me, "He'll prove them wrong." He still hasn't proved them wrong, but I think he's OK with that.

"You can't steal people's life stories for your novel."

"I'm not. I'm just using the feelings their stories give to me."

"That's so cheesy."

"I know. I sound like your mother, huh?" His voice stays steady instead of choking up at the mention of Mom, which makes me feel like I've been left behind because I still choke up at the mention of Mom and maybe this means Dad is moving on without me. If Dad is moving on that means he's really leaving me behind in the dust like he left me behind in the laurel bush. I start feeling angry, so I tell Dad I have to go because Hanna and Lyssa are coming over—even though they're not—and I hand the phone back to Grandma. She frowns at me because she knows Lyssa and Hanna aren't coming over. I shake my head at Grandma and then retreat upstairs.

In my room, I pull out a piece of paper and start copying down my list for Shannon. I make sure to add 'DAD LEAVING ME' in bold. That's definitely on The List. Grandma and Grandpa don't bother me for the rest of the night.

Summertime has always been the season for birthdays in the Summers household—every birthday but mine. A very morbid part of me is grateful, for lack of a better word, that the accident happened on June 28 because it was after Rowan's birthday (June 14) and Dad's birthday (June 25). Having all their birthdays in a row would have been too much to stomach.

Today is July 28, which means it's been a month since the accident and it's also what should have been Tansy's eleventh birthday. I almost forgot, which sounds terrible, especially considering the fact that Mom was very obsessed with birthdays. Time just feels like it isn't passing in the right order, even more so than it usually does in the summer. Some days it feels like it's been a week since June 28 and other days it feels like it's been seven years, and today does not feel like Tansy's should-be eleventh birthday at all.

Grandma and Grandpa buy a cake. Dad calls and we sing "Happy Birthday," which makes me feel so sad I hide in my room and cry. Pumpkin follows me, sits in my lap, and starts whining because maybe he's realized Mom and Tansy and Rowan aren't coming home. I'm crying the kind of tears that make it so I can't breathe, and I try to open my mouth to scream, but nothing comes out except for a whisper because I don't have enough breath in my lungs to scream. Tansy should have been eleven and gone to middle school in September and even though middle school is kind of terrible, I still wish it was something she got to experience. I'll never complain about how awkward middle school was again because at least I got to go to middle school.

When Tansy was born everyone kept calling her Pansy, even Grandma and Grandpa. Nobody knew what a tansy flower was, but everyone had heard the name Pansy before, which prompted Mom to buy baby Tansy a bright yellow shirt with a T on the front for "Tansy." Eventually, her name stuck.

Missing people is contagious, because it spreads through all the people you've ever missed. I think about Tansy and I miss her, and then I think about Mom and Rowan, and about Dad being in Kentucky. Eventually I'm thinking about my second-grade friend who moved away and the girl who used to live down the street and babysat us when we were little and the boy in the airport with the flowers in his journal and the girl with the laptop. I miss everyone. It makes me sob harder.

My phone rings and it's Hanna calling me; she asks if I want her and Lyssa to come over. I'm guessing Grandma and Grandpa told her what was going on. I nod, even though she can't see that through the phone, and somehow she knows my lack of verbal response means yes, so she tells me they're taking me to celebrate Tansy's birthday in a happy way.

Singing "Happy Birthday" was supposed to be celebrating in a happy way, but that still made me sad. I keep confusing happy things with sad things, and I wonder if I'll ever go back to normal or if I'll forever cry when people sing "Happy Birthday" or when a funny episode of *Friends* comes on television.

Grandma and Grandpa let Hanna and Lyssa up to my room. Lyssa is holding a piece of the birthday cake on a plate and offers me a bite. Hanna rolls her eyes and says, "Lyssa didn't make it one step into the house before getting side-tracked by the cake."

That makes me laugh. Lyssa grins with cake in her teeth and says, "Hey, why would I turn down free cake?"

Lyssa is very good at joking when things are sad. I let Lyssa stuff cake into my mouth, and Hanna goes into the bathroom to get a wet washcloth for me. "Cold water will make the swelling in your eyes go down. It'll help with that feeling in your face after crying where your skin feels all tight."

"Really?"

"Yes. You know, sometimes my knowledge is useful."

"Emphasis on sometimes," Lyssa mutters. She has cake in her mouth so it sounds more like "shomtimes," which makes us giggle.

Grandma and Grandpa are standing in the doorway. "This is what we should be doing," Grandma says. "Laughing. Tansy would have wanted us laughing."

Hanna glances at me like she's afraid I'm going to burst into tears because Grandma said Tansy's name, but that doesn't happen. Like I said, all the things that should be sad and the things that should be happy have gotten mixed up in my brain.

I stick my hand into my pocket and feel for the pressed not-tansy. Oddly enough, I don't feel Ghost Tansy near me, which makes me feel a bit sad because it's her birthday and I should be feeling her more today than usual. Instead, all I feel is the pressed flower in my pocket that may or may not be a tansy.

"Yeah. She would want us to be laughing," I reply. Hanna smiles at me but still looks like she's worried I won't be OK. Lyssa forces cake into my mouth and says, "Eat!"

After a while, Lyssa and Hanna say they want to take me to the mountains. Grandpa offers to drive us even though he hates driving on the freeway, which is very nice of him. I want to tell him he doesn't have to, mostly because I don't want Grandma to be home alone. I know being home alone can make a person very sad.

"Oh, I'll be fine here," Grandma Lucy tells us. "Go!"

I can't wait until January when Hanna is the first one to turn sixteen and she's able to legally drive us everywhere. She has her permit and is a very good driver already, which isn't surprising, because she's good at paying attention. When Rowan got his license, Dad was terrified. Mom said she trusted him, and Mom was right because Rowan turned out to be a very good driver. It surprised all of us but Mom, who said Rowan was good at paying attention to things when he wanted to. Mom always said I was the one to look out for because my head was up in the clouds. Dad would say, "Laurel is our rational one!" And Mom would say, "That's what she wants you to think."

I'm not sure what I wanted them to think. I just wanted to be Laurel—just Laurel.

Hanna says we are going to the pass where people ski in the winter because there should be tansy flowers there. She sits in the front seat and gives Grandpa driving directions and helps him change lanes because that's the part of driving on the freeway he hates the most.

The freeway makes me nervous because the cars could swerve at any second and crush us all like Mom and Tansy and Rowan. Part of me thinks that wouldn't be so bad because then I'd be with Mom and Tansy and Rowan, and another part of me knows it would be very bad because then Dad and Grandma would be all alone and so would Mr. and Mrs. Jackson and Lyssa's foster parents, who she doesn't like to talk about very often.

Lyssa can tell I'm feeling anxious because she glances over at me and then announces that she wants to play a game.

"What game?"

"Name three fictional characters that, when combined together, would make up your personality."

"That's not a game. That's a question."

"Thanks for your insight, Hanna. Just for that, I've decided that one of your characters is Squidward Tentacles."

"From *SpongeBob*?"

"That's the one."

"Great."

Lyssa sticks her tongue out at Hanna and then continues. "I'll go first. I would be…hmm…Mulan. I want to be Mulan."

"Ooh, that's a good one!"

"And Harry Potter. Because of the whole orphan-with-a-tragic-life thing. Hey, Laurel, you could be Harry now too!"

Hanna tenses up in the seat in front of me.

"We should start a club."

"A genius idea, dear Laurel."

Grandpa isn't paying attention to our conversation because he's concentrating so hard on the road. "You're good to switch over," Hanna tells him. He changes lanes, and I swallow hard to keep my nerves down. Lyssa keeps talking. "I think my third character would be April Ludgate from *Parks and Rec*. Obviously because of my previously demonstrated dark sense of humor."

"Honestly, that's pretty accurate," Hanna comments.

"Now you go! Except you only get to name two because Squidward is one of them."

"I hate you."

"You love me."

"If you're April, can I be Leslie Knope?"

"You're not nice enough to be her. You don't care enough about people."

"Hey!"

I stare out the window and watch the trees pass by. I fade in and out of the conversation because I start trying to think about what characters I would be, and I can't think of any. Mom always told me I was sensitive and thoughtful, and Dad always said I was responsible and funny, but Rowan said I was annoying, and Tansy said I was silly. I can't be all of those things at once—it would be too conflicting. All the things I've ever been are the things people told me I was, and now that I've lost most of my people, I'm not sure who I am anymore.

Lyssa and Hanna settle on Hermione Granger and Elsa from *Frozen* for Hanna, because she is very studious and also cold toward people she doesn't know. I tell them they can decide for me. Lyssa protests—"That's not how the game works!"—but then they launch into an in-depth discussion of what characters I would be. Lyssa suggests that I would be Donkey from *Shrek*, which makes me laugh so hard my side aches. Hanna says I remind her of the little sister from *The Lion, the Witch and the Wardrobe*. The little sister used to always remind me of Tansy, but I don't say that out loud because I don't want to make all of us sad.

When we get to the parking lot at the pass, Grandpa turns around and says, "Don't ever grow up and become boring, girls."

"I fully intend to stay fifteen forever," Lyssa replies.

"Too late. I've already become boring," Hanna mutters.

"Everyone thinks they're boring."

"I don't! I think I'm exciting!" Lyssa smiles. I wonder if there's a part of her that does worry that she's boring. Lyssa is the least boring person I know, and for the record, Hanna is one of the other least boring people I know, though I'd never admit it to her.

Hanna says that tansy flowers grow on the side of the road sometimes. She also says we probably didn't have to drive out so far, but she knows for sure they grow at the pass so that's why we did. We wander around the parking lot and search where the pavement meets the dirt until we find a patch of yellow flowers (or as the flower-shop boy would call them, "weeds"). Hanna gets tears in her eyes and Grandpa takes a picture on his old-fashioned flip phone to show my grandma. They look similar to the pressed not-tansy—kind of. Maybe the pressed not-tansy is actually a pressed tansy.

Hanna asks me if I want to take one home.

"No," I say. "I want it to grow." That feels much more poetic to me. Dad would be proud. If I were to take it home, I'd have to uproot it and then it would die, eventually, which would make me very sad.

"We could press it like the other one," Hanna suggests.

"No. I like the one I have."

Another part of me doesn't want to take the tansy because it's in a patch of other tansies and I don't want to pull it apart from its family. I know it's a flower—or "weed"—and it doesn't have thoughts or feelings or a family, but I still don't want to uproot it. Lyssa bends down and kisses the yellow, sponge-like flower head. "Happy birthday, Tansy," she says, and then lets out a sneeze. "Smells like grass. Allergies." Hanna wipes her eyes and I hold her hand because I want her to know it's OK for her to grieve too and that I really didn't mean it when I said they were only mine to grieve.

"She was so beautiful," Hanna whispers. She's now properly crying, and I let her cry into my shoulder. It feels nice to be the shoulder and not the person crying for a change. I'm not even sure if Hanna cried at the funeral or if she's cried since she found out. I wonder what she was doing when she found out; I don't remember telling her or Lyssa but somehow they found out, and they both rushed over to my house to be there to watch me and Dad fall apart. It's all fuzzy in my memory, but I do remember they were there—I remember their faces and their voices.

"I hate him," Hanna whispers. "I hate that man who was driving the truck."

"Me too," Lyssa says.

I hate him too, but I don't say it out loud. I'm glad that they hate him too because now I don't feel so bad. I don't even know his name. I know somebody told me it at some point, but I don't remember a lot of things from those first few days. I know that he's going to jail because he killed my family, even though it was an accident, and that makes me sort of sad because what if he has a family too? And he's not a flower like the tansies in the ground, so uprooting him could really hurt some other people. But I still hate him. When I think about him, and how if he hadn't run that light things would be so different, my stomach gets all cramped up and I'm afraid I might throw up. I try and push him out of my thoughts, try to keep him out of my head every time we see a truck flash by on the freeway.

When we get back into the car, we have nothing more than what we came with. Maybe Lyssa and Hanna were expecting me to pick tansies and bring them home to decorate the house. That didn't happen, but it feels like something even bigger happened because Hanna cried and Lyssa wished Tansy a happy birthday and Grandpa's eyes crinkled when he smiled and told us to never grow up and get boring, and Hanna, Lyssa, and I all admitted that we hated the man who drove that truck. Grandpa drives us home and then he and Grandma take the three of us out for burgers. We don't talk about Tansy or Mom or Rowan because sometimes you need to stop talking about the sad things, and instead we let Hanna talk about the book she's reading and Lyssa talk about her favorite Netflix original show and laugh and just be light.

25

Mom's birthday is one day after Tansy's, so it was always very confusing in our household. One year, Dad got the two birthdays mixed up. But this year I want to pretend it's not happening, because it's all too much at once. I ask Grandma and Grandpa if we can wait to celebrate Mom and they say OK and that we can celebrate Mom any day and any time I want to. I'm not sure if I want to celebrate her birthday this year at all.

I text Lyssa and Hanna to tell them we are pretending my mom's birthday is not today because I can't handle another dead person's birthday. And besides, I have counseling today, so I'm already going to have to talk about things I don't want to talk about.

"Today is my mom's birthday but we aren't celebrating it because we had to celebrate Tansy's yesterday and I woke up today not wanting to celebrate things," I say to Shannon.

"That makes sense. Sometimes it's hard to celebrate things."

"Yes. Exactly. Can I tell you something?"

"Of course."

"I think I'm seeing ghosts, or more like feeling ghosts. I haven't for a few days, though, so I'm afraid that they've left me. I hear them tell me things."

"Ghosts of your mom? And Rowan and Tansy?"

"Yes."

"That's perfectly normal after experiencing a loss."

"That's what Hanna would say."

"Hanna sounds like she knows a lot about psychology."

"She knows a lot about everything."

"Did you bring that list?"

"Yes."

"Do you want to show me?"

I take the crumpled-up piece of paper out of my pocket. It's longer than the first list that Hanna started writing for me.

1. *"I'm so sorry"*
2. *My coping mechanisms*
3. *Mom and Rowan and Tansy*
4. *My dad trying to kill himself*
5. *Going back to school in September*
6. *Hanna kissing me*
7. *Dad leaving me in a bush*

Shannon reads it and then says, "I think we violated The List a couple of times today already."

"That's OK. I don't know if I even like The List anymore. It feels kind of restrictive."

"Alright then. Do you still want to try and draw out some of the things on The List?"

"I don't know."

Shannon hands me a piece of paper and some markers.

"I don't know how to draw The List. I'm not sure why I agreed to it."

Shannon nods. "You can draw whatever you want." I pick up the orange marker and start to draw, and without even thinking about it much, I start drawing Mom. I draw Ghost Mom the way she looked when she was in my room and I was having a "fever-induced hallucination" from the infected tattoo. Shannon tells me it's a really nice drawing.

"That's because my mom was very pretty."

"Do I have permission to break The List?"

"Sure."

"What was your mom like?"

"That's a very big question."

"What was your favorite thing about her, then?"

"That's also a very big question. But my answer would be her hair because it was brighter red than Rowan's and Tansy's. It was almost blinding but in a pretty way, and she was very good at braiding it. She could even French braid her hair without looking. I never figured out how to do that."

"I don't think I could do that either."

"Yeah, it's really hard. I don't know how she did it." I remember Mom's hands and how they used to run through my hair at night when she would come into my room. And then I remember how those hands were smashed to bits because of the stupid truck driver. I start feeling sad, so I flip the drawing over. Ghost Mom disappears and all that's in front of me is a blank sheet of paper. I add "Mom's hair" to The List because apparently her hair makes me sad now.

"It's OK to do that sometimes," Shannon says. "To just... flip it over, metaphorically. Let yourself stop thinking about it."

"I feel bad when I do that. Like I'm a bad person." I imagine Ghost Mom popping out of the drawing and yelling at me for flipping her over. Mom never yelled, but maybe Ghost Mom is a yeller. I keep my hand on top of the flipped-over piece of paper because I'm afraid that if I lift it, Ghost Mom will pop out.

"That's why I want you to know it's OK," Shannon replies. "It doesn't make you a bad person."

"Are you sure?"

"Yes, Laurel."

"OK." I pause for a moment and then add, "But I might be a bad person, because I hate him."

Shannon stares at me and then asks, "Who?"

"The man who drove the truck. I don't even know his name, but I hate him with all my guts, though I know I shouldn't because he might have had a family too, right? But I despise him, I really do." I've been letting it eat away at me, but saying it out loud doesn't bring the relief I'd hoped it would. I don't even have a face to match him with—I can't remember what he looks like or whether the police showed us a photograph. Everything from those first few days is a blur. But the fact that he's still out there gets to me, as if he pops up out of nowhere, like when I was dropping Dad off and all I could think about was how different things would be if he hadn't run that light.

"That's OK, Laurel," Shannon tells me.

"Stop telling me that it's OK—it's not OK." I stand, because suddenly there's this surge of energy that courses through my veins and I don't want to stay still and talk about my feelings. I want to find him, at least find his name, and tell him what he did, how badly he messed up my entire family.

"Laurel," Shannon says. "We still have twenty minutes."

"I don't feel very good right now."

"If you need to go home, that's OK. We'll just want to make sure that your grandfather is here to get you."

"OK. He's out front I bet. He just waits here while I do this."

I know Grandpa isn't out front because he told me that today he'd be at the grocery store until the end of my appointment, but I want to get out of here as fast as possible so I can find out the name. The police station isn't far from my counselor's office. I could make it there and back before Grandpa even knew.

"I'll see you next week!" I say, so fast it sounds like one word all together, and then I bolt out the door and leave Shannon sitting there with a somewhat disgruntled expression on her face. I hope I haven't completely ruined being a therapist for her.

I tear down the streets, awkwardly running as fast as I can to the police station that's nearly a mile away, south toward the city and away from home, because all I can think about is the man who drove the truck and how I don't know his name—I'm not even certain that it was a man, it could have been a woman. I know nothing about him, but I hate him. My feet hit the pavement and I pass laurel bush after laurel bush. They line the hedges of the nearby houses, their leaves decorating the sidewalks and the streets, which makes me even angrier.

I throw open the door to the police station and, between pants, speak to the woman at the counter. "I need to…I need to know who killed my mom."

26

His name is Walter Redding and he used to live in Shoreline, just next to the courthouse, with his elderly mother. Now he's in a correctional center in downtown Seattle, just a bus ride away from where I live, awaiting his official court date. That's all the information I get before they call Grandpa and get him to come pick me up.

Grandpa doesn't lecture me about the whole debacle. He just mutters, "I won't tell Grandma," and we both agree that's the best course of action. Mentally, I pledge to do as much research on Walter Redding as I possibly can over the next few days because I need to know more about this man I hate. He worked for a shipment company for a grocery store and was driving one of those large white trucks full of bulk food. My mom and siblings were killed by a glorified food truck. It makes me sick to my stomach.

"There's someone here waiting for you," Grandma says, and I try my best to hide the determined look on my face and hope she can't see through Grandpa's stern expression. Grandma nods up toward my room, which means it's either Lyssa or Hanna or both of them.

It's Lyssa. She's sitting on my bed and asks, "Where were you?"

"Counseling."

"Hmm."

I'm not lying—I *was* at counseling. I also sort of freaked out and ran to the police station to get a name I've already been told multiple times, though it never stuck in my brain. "What's up?" I ask Lyssa, though deep down, I want her to leave so I can properly research this guy.

"I wanted to tell you…I wasn't at work today, I was actually at a meeting. With my foster parents."

"OK?"

She smiles even wider, like there's something inside of her she can't keep in. "They're adopting me, Laurel."

Her smile is contagious. It spreads to my face and for a moment, I forget all about Walter Redding and his stupid truck. Instead, I let Lyssa's grin light up the room. "Really?"

"Yeah. They told me this morning and we were just meeting with my social worker to go over some of the paperwork. Like, it's really, really happening."

"Oh my gosh." I give Lyssa a hug and her warmth spreads into my body. The air between us is less like thick sand—it feels like the world's resistance against my every move begins to dissipate.

"I wanted to tell you first, because you already met my foster mom. She seemed nice, right? Like, she'll be a good mom?"

"She seemed awesome. She didn't judge me for my hot yoga–induced mental breakdown about the floor."

"OK, good. Just wanted to check. Get the Laurel stamp of approval."

"Are you going to tell Hanna?"

"Yes, yes, I will. I want you both to come to my adoption court date. I get to dress all nice and get paperwork signed and then I'm officially Lyssa James-Burman instead of Lyssa James, orphan."

"That has a nice ring to it. We'll be there. I'll force Hanna to cancel all her other plans."

"I just…I didn't think…I don't know. I always thought I was too old to get adopted."

"You're fifteen. That's three more years until you're legally an adult."

"I don't know. Three years goes by quickly."

"Can we meet them? Like, properly meet them instead of your foster mom unknowingly comforting me at that yoga studio?"

Lyssa laughs and says, "Of course." Then she gets up and turns on music and does a sort of happy dance around the room. "I'm never going to get old and boring!" she exclaims. "And I'm never going to have to move around again!"

It feels good to have something happy to think about. I flip over the metaphorical piece of paper and stop thinking about Mom and Rowan and Tansy and dance with Lyssa in my bedroom.

Bad things keep happening all around us but we're giggling and dancing right now, and maybe the real reason we keep going is for the people who dance with us and hold us close and let us cry and feed us cake when we're upset. I swear, Ghost Mom dances around the room with us. Even though I'm not thinking about her and how it's her birthday, I believe she'd say that smiling about Lyssa getting adopted and dancing around my bedroom is the best way to celebrate.

Lyssa proceeds to launch into a conversation about how her new parents met, which was apparently on a cruise to Alaska. Penny was with her parents and Sanjay was with his sister and they were staying in rooms right next to one another. Penny has never wanted to be pregnant, she's always wanted to adopt, and Sanjay thinks that adopting is better because there are a lot of kids in the world without parents. Penny's parents were apparently really mad at first because they wanted her to have biological kids and told her that adopting just "isn't the same." Penny didn't speak to her parents for three years after that, but they've just started talking again and Lyssa is going to meet them soon. She's already met Sanjay's parents, who are apparently very nice.

"Why didn't you want to talk about them before?" I ask her.

"I didn't want to tell you and Hanna about them because…I didn't want you to get excited if it wasn't going to be—*you know*. I've gotten close to getting adopted before. The last time, they changed their minds because the mom lost her job and they decided they couldn't afford me. After that I dyed my hair for the first time."

"You're such a cliché. Dyeing your hair after every major life change."

"Don't drag me like that. It's cathartic, OK?"

We laugh and she says, "I'm going to tell Hanna now. Do you want to come with me?"

A feeling rises from my stomach to my chest, as if the happiness of Lyssa's news disappears and I remember what was happening before I got home, how I ran to the police station and how much I hate the truck driver, Walter Redding.

"I'm kind of tired. I had a long day."

Lyssa shrugs. "Alright. But you guys will come with me to pick out a dress, right? My court date is in a little over a week. You better be there. Not like you have much else to do."

"Moping around takes up most of my schedule."

"Like a bruised vegetable." She winks at me, throws her arms around me, and then bounds down the stairs and lets herself out. For a moment, I bask in her happiness—but time passes, and it turns sour inside of me. Because deep down, I'm still angry—I'm happy and angry at the same time.

Once I'm all alone in my room, I look up the distance toward the correctional center. By bus, it's about forty minutes on a weekday. I try to imagine myself going there—sweet little Laurel standing in a jail, talking to the man who killed my mom from across one of those glass windows with the phones, like in all the movies and cop shows I've ever watched. Grandma and Grandpa would be shocked. But if I do it, it has to be soon—Dad's coming home in two weeks, and Lyssa's court date is just before that. Everything is going to change soon, and I feel unresolved, like pieces of me are still floating in the air like ghosts. Maybe it'll always be that way.

I know everyone in my life would tell me visiting Walter Redding was a bad idea, and I've never visited a jail before and I don't know what kind of security I'll be up against. "I shouldn't," I whisper to myself. Downstairs, I hear Pumpkin yip and Grandma bustling around, saying, "I'll feed you in a second, buddy."

But that's all wrong, because Grandma doesn't know that Pumpkin always eats at the same time as us—it used to be Mom's rule. She said she wanted him to feel like a member of the family, eating his food out of his bowl as we all sat around the dinner table. Mom's not here to tell her she's doing it all wrong, and this is going to become the new normal, because Mom won't ever be here to tell her. Pumpkin will just get used to eating all by himself and it's all because of Walter Redding.

I save the bus route and then I close my laptop and wander downstairs.

The bus is rickety and packed heading down to the middle of the city. Grandma and Grandpa think I'm at Lyssa's house to help her get ready for her big day, and Lyssa and Hanna think I had plans with my grandparents this morning. Maybe doing this on the same day as Lyssa's adoption service wasn't such a good idea. But, according to my map and my estimate of no more than an hour confronting Walter Redding, I should be back in Shoreline by 2:00 p.m., and Lyssa's hearing is at 3:00 p.m. Which *should* give me enough time, assuming I don't get kidnapped, murdered, or stuck in terrible traffic.

As the sun rises, it shines in through the window and makes me sweat in my sticky seat. I wonder where everyone else is going—likely off to work, or to visit family. I highly doubt they too are traveling to the county jail to visit the man who killed their family. If that's the case, then the world is even more broken than I thought.

The trees rush by the window in brilliant, indistinguishable shades of green, and I wonder how many laurel bushes we've passed on this bus—probably hundreds just in the time I've been on it. With every truck we pass, I wonder whether Walter Redding would have driven it if he hadn't hit my family.

But as we approach the city, the colors beside the freeway all fade together and the towering buildings loom into view.

When I glance down at my phone, I see Hanna has asked me what time I'm going over to Lyssa's. I tell her not until later and leave out the part about me heading downtown to confront the man who killed my family. If I let that slip to Hanna, she'd have a heart attack. And besides, I can barely say it out loud to myself—it feels ridiculous. I have no plan. As the minutes pass on the hot, sweaty bus, I start to worry maybe this wasn't such a good idea. But I tell myself if I don't confront him now, maybe I never will, and it might be one of those things I regret forever.

Eventually, after nearly twenty minutes of stopping at light after light on the crowded streets, the bus pulls over to my stop and I file out of it, along with a handful of other passengers in suits with briefcases, ready for their workdays. I swallow hard, ignoring the knot in my stomach and squinting into the sun. The sun is fully in the middle of the sky, the heat shining down on my back as I step off the bus and onto the sidewalk. According to my phone, it's a 0.2-mile walk from the bus stop to the correctional center, and I need to walk fast because I have limited time and have to be back to the bus stop by 1:00 p.m.

I don't know what I'm doing—panic fills my chest, because what am I supposed to say to the guy? Do they even allow kids to visit people in prison they have no relation to? What if they ask questions and then stare at me like I'm insane because I'm here to visit the man who killed my mom and siblings? Maybe I should lie—say I'm his kid, or something. Though I don't think he has kids, because when I looked him up I saw that he lived with his mom and that was it, so they probably wouldn't believe me. Maybe I could say I'm a family friend, or a niece, though I'm not sure if he had any siblings, so they might see through that lie too. Maybe

I should turn around and go back. I shake my head—the thought of returning makes me feel worse, because there's so much anger buried deep down in me. I have to try and see him, try and talk to him, and if I get dragged out for yelling at him, then at least I tried.

From the outside, the building looks just like all the other buildings in the city: tall and filled with windows, people dressed in nice clothes bustling in and out of it. It's not how I expected a jail to look—no tall walls or fences lining the entirety of the building. Instead of making me feel frozen, like it normally does, the anxious feeling in my chest makes me walk faster, fueling my legs and bringing me closer and closer to the building. I slip in through the double doors behind a group of people and notice the armed policeman standing near the door, with his black uniform and stern face. For a moment I freeze—he makes me feel nervous. But then my body keeps moving, and I puff my chest out and walk up to him. "I'm here to visit someone," I say, looking him in the eye and hoping he won't ask any more questions. He's taller than me, much taller, and the gun on his belt makes me want to run and hide.

"Did you schedule a visit?" he asks in a deep, gruff voice.

I swallow hard. I didn't know I needed to schedule a visit—in all the movies I've ever seen, they just walk right in, sit behind the glass, and yell. That's what I pictured: me sitting on the other side of the glass, telling him how much he had ruined my life.

"You've got to schedule a visit," the officer continues.

Another officer has walked up beside him, this one a woman, and she frowns at me. "Are you eighteen or older?"

"N—no." My voice shakes. I don't want to cry, not here in front of the intense looking officers, but the way he's staring at me reminds me of that first day at the station after the accident—the disjointed memories of the police telling me what happened. "We're so sorry," they said. "Who did it?" Dad asked. And then they must have said his name, though the memory feels blurry, and they asked if we'd press charges and Dad hung his head low.

"You have to have an adult with you if you're under eighteen," says the woman, her voice snapping me back into focus as I will the tears to stay in my eyes. "What's your name?"

My voice freezes in my throat—I don't know if I should lie, or if I should tell them the truth. All I know is I want to see him so I can yell at him and tell him he ruined my family, he ruined my life, he made my dad try to kill himself and now I'm seeing ghosts and everything is wrong, upside down.

"What's your name, kid?"

"He killed my mom." The words fall out and then suddenly I can't stop them, couldn't even if I tried: a waterfall of words that I shouldn't be speaking, yet here I am. "He killed my mom and my brother and sister and I need to see him so that I can tell him what he did. He doesn't know, he has no way of knowing how bad it's been. My dad tried to kill himself and I just want to tell Walter Redding how terrible he is because nothing is the same, because he ran that red light, and he smashed them into bits." I'm yelling now, and I try to push past them but they grab hold of my arms and say, "You need an adult with you," which is the least useful thing they could possibly say, so I kick and yell, "I don't have an adult! Let me see him! Let me see him, I came all the way up here, let me tell him how terrible he is! Please, let me through!"

"Where are your parents?"

I gape at the officers, because I *just* told them that Mom was dead and Dad tried to kill himself, all because of Walter Redding, who is in the same building as me right now, but I can't see him. And then I keep yelling. "Let me through! Please! Let me through!"

"We're going to need to call your parents."

"You can't! You can't call them, because of Walter Redding!"

"Where is your legal guardian?" At least he doesn't say parents this time. The panic has now filled my entire body, and I feel sweet, quiet Laurel Summers disappear. I aim a kick at his shin and then I run out the door and down the street, my feet slapping against the pavement. What am I going to do if they go after me? What am I going to tell my grandparents?

But they don't go after me. I realize this after I've made it about three blocks and nearly run into several children. They don't care. I'm not a threat, I'm just a kid—a kid who started crying and screaming at police officers. They're probably just standing near the entrance with dumbstruck expressions, caught somewhere between annoyance and pity. Maybe this is just a typical day for them. Maybe I'm nothing more than another crying kid.

With the sun pounding on my back, I walk toward the bus stop.

When the bus heading north pulls up to the stop, I duck my head and squeeze inside, finding a seat squished against the window. Tears blur my vision as I head back home, so this time I don't have to see all the stupid trees or wonder about the stupid laurel bushes as we move away from the center of the city. Away from Walter Redding.

At least I know I won't be late for Lyssa's adoption.

It's not until we get much closer to home that I remember what I have in my pocket. I pull it out and look down—it's a slip of paper from the police station back home with two addresses on it. The first is the correctional center and the second is Walter Redding's address from when he lived with his mom and was yet to be an inmate, awaiting his trial.

I clutch it in my hands and my vision turns red. I'll go to his house. It's right across from the Shoreline District Court, where I'm supposed to meet Lyssa and her family. If I can't talk to him, I'll talk to his mom. I'll make her schedule me a visitation appointment and maybe I'll even make her go with me, as my adult supervision, and then I'll go up there and tell him what he did, and I'll make him feel bad. I'll make him feel all the things I've been feeling and then some.

By the time the bus stops, my tears have dried, and I have two hours until Lyssa's adoption service. I can make it in time, I know I can.

The Redding house, conveniently, is only a few blocks away from the downtown court. It's not so much a house as a tiny townhome tucked between a dozen other tiny townhomes, with flowers in the yard and a cat sitting on the doorstep. I stand outside, my body slumped over, my eyes still red and puffy, and stare at it like a zombie. Finally, I see her.

She's crouched down in the garden, wearing all green so she nearly blends in with the shrubs and the leaves. She has white hair and glasses on her face, and even from across the street, I hear her humming a song. She looks like a normal old lady, except I know she's not normal, because her son killed my mom and siblings, and he needs to know how badly he messed up.

I cross the street and clear my throat. She doesn't seem to hear me—she just continues tending to her plants. They're beautiful. It's a garden Mom would have been proud of. How ironic—Mom would have loved the garden in the yard of the man who killed her.

"Hi," I say. She glances up, her eyes wide, and then gives me a large smile. "Oh, hello, dear. Is that Marnie? From down the street?"

"My name is Laurel."

She walks over to me slowly, hobbling, leaning against a walker. Her eyes are kind, much kinder than I would have expected. "Laurel, Laurel...do I know you?"

I can see the strain of forgetfulness in her face, the way her forehead crinkles and she looks frustrated, as she tries to place my face. "Not really," I say.

"Would you like to see my garden?" her voice is soft, like a song, and free. "My son likes to help me, but he hasn't been coming around much." It's like she doesn't even know what happened to her son—what he did.

I want to tell her that her son is in jail for killing my family, but then I look at her—soft, wrinkled, smiling, and I can't bring myself to do it. The anger inside of me falls away; the vision of me yelling at her son through a glass window disappears and crumples into a million pieces at my feet. Instead, I just feel like breaking apart myself, because the way she stares at her plants reminds me of Mom. I don't want to be angry, I just want Mom.

"Come on. Here, these are the peonies..." I follow her and crouch in her yard, marveling at the innocence in her eyes, the ability to invite a stranger into her home in the middle of a relatively busy city, across from a courthouse where, in just a few hours, Lyssa will find her own home. The smell of flowers fills my nose and I sneeze, which makes her laugh. "And here are the roses," she's saying, as if I've never seen a rose before. I follow her all over her garden until the tour comes to an end and my phone buzzes with messages from Lyssa and Hanna.

Mrs. Redding lets me take a flower with me. When I stand to leave, she has a confused expression on her face, like she's forgotten who I am, who she is. Growing old sounds terrifying. "Are you a friend of my son?" she asks.

I shake my head no. "Just Laurel."

"I'll see you around, Laurel."

"Sure."

She's so nice that I wonder if maybe he was nice too. Or if at least a part of him was nice. Maybe he wasn't bad after all, and it's for the best that I didn't yell at him. What if it was all really an accident, which makes it all the more tragic—because who am I supposed to blame then? The universe? Mom always said the universe worked in magical ways, though I'm having trouble believing that nowadays. I feel sad, but I also feel lighter inside.

I walk down the street like I'm emerging from a bad dream, hopping back into reality and the smiling faces of my friends. The bustle of the courthouse makes me feel like an outsider, the world moving quickly around me, cases being settled—ruining and saving lives simultaneously. I find Hanna and Mr. and Mrs. Jackson amidst the chaos of it all, all dressed nice with flowers in their hands.

"Is that for Lyssa?" Hanna asks me, nodding at the peony from Mrs. Redding that I'm clutching. I realize I never even got her first name—I don't know that I ever will.

I nod. "Just picked it."

"It's pretty." Hanna smiles and I walk in with her family. I'll tell her about my day later, when we're alone, but for now, it feels like something that was just for me. It's like a piece of myself has returned as I clutch the flower to my chest and think about how strange it is that there are so many good people in the world and so many bad people, and somehow, we all coexist. And the bad people aren't always that bad all the time, they just do bad things.

The courtroom is much smaller than I expected, filled with a few wooden pews and bright white lights that hurt my head to look at. The judge sits at the front, a tall woman with a huge smile on her face. I think that if I were to be a judge, I'd want to be a judge that handles happy cases, like Lyssa getting adopted, instead of a judge in the movies who has to watch murder trial after murder trial. In the front pew, Lyssa sits with Sanjay and Penny. We file in behind them and I squeeze Lyssa on the shoulder.

Hanna and I get to sit and watch as they declare Lyssa a child of Penny and Sanjay. It feels like something that shouldn't have to be in a courtroom because courtrooms always make me feel uneasy (probably because of all the crime shows I've watched), but the judge has such a nice smile that it almost doesn't feel like some weird legal proceeding. Both Penny and Sanjay cry, and even Lyssa tears up as she shakes the judge's hand. Hanna and I clap and take pictures of them afterward, and Penny and Sanjay kiss each other and put their arms around Lyssa and she looks so happy it makes me cry. I stand there outside the courtroom with tears dripping down my face and onto the marble floor beneath us. Hanna asks, "Are you OK?"

"I'm happy-crying," I tell her, "which is a nice change."

She takes my hand in hers and leans her head against my shoulder. It's making my feelings jumbled up again, and Hanna's hand shakes, so maybe her feelings are jumbled up too.

Death is weird, because when people die happy things continue to happen in the world and they start to feel wrong, even though they're not.

"I'm so happy," Lyssa tells us. She's wearing this big smile on her face, but she looks slightly nervous too. "Is it OK if I'm happy?" She looks at me like she's asking for permission.

"Are you not supposed to be?" I ask.

"Well, it just feels…like you lost your family and I finally got one. And I know it's not connected but I feel like it's not allowed. Or more like, it's unfair. It's completely unfair."

"I'm happy," I tell her, "for you."

"Can a person be this happy when they're also so sad?" she asks.

"I think so."

"I guess we're finding out as we go."

Hanna starts talking about how emotions are complex and how they aren't exclusive from one another. Lyssa tells her to shut up and take a break from being a walking encyclopedia. Hanna looks like she's about to retort but then Penny and Sanjay put their arms around Lyssa and we all end up laughing because things are so happy even though they're also so sad.

Grandma Lucy tells me I'm too young to have to think about all these things at once, but I still have to think about them—and by association, so do Hanna and Lyssa. I should probably feel guilty for dragging them into this, but this situation dragged me in, and they're always going to follow where I go and save me. I'm the sinking anchor, and they're the people on the boat who reel me back in and get me to shore.

Afterward, Lyssa, Penny, and Sanjay go to lunch. "Do you want to come?" they ask me and Hanna.

Hanna looks like she's about to say yes, but I feel the tiredness in my body and the weight of my morning journey hitting me so hard that I interrupt her. "I think I should go home," I say. Hanna frowns at me, and I add, "You guys should go enjoy your day together, as a family." I smile, but deep down, the words sting. Because now Lyssa has a family and I've lost mine. It's a cruel joke on the part of the universe. I'm happy for her, but I'm also sad for me.

"Want company?" Hanna asks me. I shrug my shoulders, and she knows me well enough to take that as a yes. We congratulate the new little family, and then the two of us make our way back to my house in silence—hopping on the bus to get us out of downtown. The sinking feeling fills my stomach, the image of Lyssa standing with her new parents haunting my mind. It's all mixed in with Walter Redding, who I never got to meet, and his mother with her flowers in her garden, just like my own mother. I'm so lost in my thoughts that Hanna has to grab me by the elbow and nearly drag me off the bus when we reach our stop.

"I think I understand what Lyssa was talking about," Hanna tells me, once we're both upstairs in my room and sitting cross-legged on the floor, her with a book on her lap and me scrolling through photos on my phone.

"What do you mean?"

"About feeling like...like I'm not allowed to be happy and sad at the same time."

"Yeah?"

"Yeah. I know I talked all about how emotions aren't exclusive from one another, but I feel it too, like I'm not allowed to be happy," she says.

"That's all the more reason to be happy."

"You think so?"

"That's what Mom would say. I don't know if I personally think so. But she believed it."

"Well then, what do you think?"

"That it's OK to feel weird things when you're sad. Like sometimes I think Rowan was kind of a jerk, but then I tell myself I'm not allowed to think that because he's dead. And Tansy was always better at things than me even though she was younger. And I was mad at her for that when she was alive. And this really messed-up part of me is hoping that now I can be my dad's favorite, but I don't think I can, because he left me."

Hanna looks like she might cry; her lip quivers slightly and she fidgets with her hands, staring down at the floor. "Rowan was a jerk. I can confirm that."

"Remember when he cut off our hair when you were sleeping over here?"

"Completely psychotic."

"But I loved him."

"Me too."

"He was just angry."

"I wish I knew why."

"Maybe there wasn't an answer."

She nods and goes back to reading her book, but she's not really reading because her eyes aren't moving—they're just staring at the page. She looks up at me and says, "And…I don't think parents have a favorite child. I don't think it's possible."

"You're an only child so you wouldn't know that."

"I know your dad loves you."

"He left me."

"That doesn't mean he doesn't love you."

I guess she has a point, but I still feel very angry about Dad leaving, like I'll never get over it. Even though he'll be back soon and things will fall back into place and we'll watch TV together and laugh—I might still always be angry at him. That makes me angry at my anger, and I've dealt with enough anger for one day.

Hanna sighs and puts her book down. "I don't like this."

"Don't like what?"

She stands up and sits on my bed across from me. She looks like she's fishing for words, which is unusual for Hanna because she's always full of words. If she had been in Mom's car that day, she wouldn't have broken into bones and blood—she'd have broken into words. It's a very morbid thought, but Shannon says it's normal to think morbid things when people die in a morbid way, so maybe I'll be thinking about my friends getting hit by trucks for the rest of my life.

Hanna finally gets words out. "I messed this all up."

"What are you talking about?"

"Us. I messed us all up. I had to—I just…"

I realize what she's talking about—it dawns on me, suddenly. "*You* kissed me."

"Exactly. I messed it all up."

"I don't think you did."

She leans in and presses her forehead against mine. I can feel her breath on my face, and everything in my head seems to disappear except for her—right in front of me. "Hanna," I say. I can feel her start to shake, so I close the gap and let our lips touch just for a millisecond, so quickly that later tonight I'll probably wonder if it even happened. She's soft and I'm soft and afterward, we stay frozen with our foreheads touching. I watch as Hanna closes her eyes really tight. "I'm not ready," she whispers.

"I know."

"Things are too…"

"Jumbled?"

"Yes. Jumbled. Ouch."

Maybe a lot of fifteen-year-olds don't feel ready. Everyone seems like all they want is a boyfriend or girlfriend, but relationships end and that's scary when you're fifteen and you've just lost your family and you're in love with your best friend.

"Can we…can we just wait?"

"Yeah. Yes. Please."

Grief is the kind of thing that stomps all over love. But so do moms who tell their daughters who they can and cannot love. So do people like Rowan, who told me that being gay wasn't a big deal anymore even though it still feels like a very big deal to me, and how would he have known?

Love doesn't stomp back. It just waters it all down, like the way Mom would water the flowers in our garden and pull out all the weeds until eventually, beautiful things started to grow. I tell Hanna that I'm thinking about Mom, and she holds me and so does Ghost Mom, and maybe this is enough for me. Maybe it's OK if Dad left me because I still have a person and a ghost holding me up.

I fall asleep like that and I don't wake up until Grandpa knocks on my door. "Laurel," he says. Hanna is still sitting on my bed with her book in her hands. "A package came for you. From—well, all the way from the UK. Did you order something?"

I practically knock Hanna off the bed and go flying to grab the package.

29

For Laurel Summers—

I found your tree. You're lucky I was already planning to go on one of those bus tours up to the Highlands because I saw plenty of your trees, growing natively and all. I even asked the tour guide to make sure. I know I said that we all have dead people, but we really shouldn't. I hate that it's that way, so I felt like I owed you this for saying those things to you.

I just took a leaf from the ground. I hope that's OK. It took me forever to find somewhere to laminate it. My roommate here probably thinks I'm a weirdo for doing all this for some kid I met in an airport.

The tour guide saw me take a leaf and he told me a lot of random facts about this damn tree. Turns out it grows in the States too, if you know where to look, but I guess it's native to Europe and Asia. I'm saying that because if you looked hard enough you probably could have found it not far from where you live. It definitely grows in Washington. Which is funny. Yet I'm still sending it to you. Even though you could do this all yourself. I guess I have a stronger sense of duty than I thought I did.

Well, I hope you have a good life. I really do, that wasn't sarcastic. Sorry you've got dead people. Sorry we've both got dead people. If I ever see you again, I'll tell you about mine. But I probably won't see you again, and even if I do, you won't look the same anymore, or I won't look the same, or you won't want to hear about my dead people. So, really—have a good life.

By the way, my name is Dany.

From all the way in Scotland,
Danielle M.

The leaf looks like any other leaf. It's green and the edges are spiky, like somebody cut the leaf out with those edger scissors Mom used when she decorated scrapbooks. It's pressed just like the maybe-not-tansy, something Hanna or Dad would love to use as a bookmark.

"I wish she'd left her last name," Hanna mutters after reading the letter. "Then we could have found her and thanked her."

"I don't think she was looking for gratitude." I remember her, the girl in the airport with the laptop who looked so incredibly annoyed when I bothered her, who told me everyone had dead people, and then later apologized for saying that in a letter all the way from Scotland. I've never known anybody like that.

Grandpa asks me, "What is it?"

"It's a leaf from a rowan tree."

That makes him say "Oh" very quietly and tear up.

"I've seen this before," Hanna says. She's staring at the leaf and holding it up to the light.

"Well, apparently they grow here too. So, I bothered this girl for nothing."

"She still did it for you. That was nice of her."

"It's kind of funny."

I hold the pressed rowan-tree leaf next to the pressed maybe-not-tansy. I should start a collection of pressed flowers. They look beautiful, and when I hold them up to my window the light shines through and the yellow in the maybe-tansy sparkles. Mom and Tansy would have loved it. Rowan would have rolled his eyes, but when he thought nobody was watching, he would have taken his namesake leaf and looked at it carefully.

I would have been watching him—I was always looking and watching and seeing all the things my siblings didn't want me to see. Mom used to joke that I'd grown eyes in the back of my head. Tansy would say, "But I thought that only happened to moms!" Rowan would snicker and try to hide how much he adored Tansy and the silly things she always said. He was very bad at hiding it.

"I miss them."

"Me too."

"We could go on another adventure," Hanna suggests. "We could try and find a rowan tree here."

"I like my leaf from Scotland."

"And you like the tansy that might not be a tansy."

"I still don't believe that boy from the flower shop."

"He was rude."

Grandpa is still standing in my doorway and staring at the leaf in my hand. He doesn't seem to be listening, because if he was, he would ask us what boy we were talking about. "I'm going to give these to Dad," I tell him.

"I...yes, he'll like that."

"Did you know?" I ask. Grandpa frowns at me. "Did you know that's what he was looking for? That's why he disappeared into the forest. Because he wanted to find a rowan tree and a tansy. He was wandering around looking for them out there, all by himself. He didn't tell me until I dropped him off in Kentucky."

Grandma is in my doorway now too. Grandpa stares at me with an unreadable expression and Grandma shakes her head and says, "Your dad went into the forest because he was sad."

"And he thought that finding them would make it better."

"He must have."

"So this will make it better. It has to."

Grandma and Grandpa both look at me with very sad eyes. Even Hanna looks concerned, though I guess she always looks kind of concerned. She bites her lip and frowns.

"I don't know, Laurel," Grandma says. "But it will make him happy and a bit sad too." I'm learning that apparently, getting better isn't the same thing as being happy. A person can be very far from better and very happy at the same time.

"He's going to love it," Hanna reassures me.

Grandpa starts to cry. "Laurel, you are the most beautiful of us all." He takes the pressed plants in his hands and turns them over, again and again. The expression on his face is as though he's looking at the most beautiful piece of artwork in the world. I have this theory that when people get old the world either makes them hard or soft. Grandma has become hard—she frowns when she's upset, and she purses her lips like she's trying to hold everything inside. And she always says "We'll keep going" and "Chin up" like a warrior. Grandpa has become soft— he has crinkles around his eyes, and he gives me more hugs than he used to when I was a little kid. I love Grandma very much, but I hope I become soft like Grandpa when I'm old.

I always thought Mom was the soft one and Dad was the hard one, or at least, that was the direction they were heading. But Dad was the one who went missing in a forest trying to find a flower and a tree and Dad is the one who has broken into a billion pieces, so maybe he's the soft one, after all. I'm not sure what Mom would have done, if she was the one who got left behind.

A part of me doesn't want to give the pressed leaves to Dad. I want to keep them for myself. The pressed maybe-not-tansy has grown a home in my pocket, and I don't want it to feel like I've abandoned it. And yes, I *know* it's a flower, a dead flower for that matter, and it doesn't have feelings or any sort of attachment to my pocket. I'll still feel guilty. I remind myself that Dad went missing for days because he couldn't find these plants so he might need them more than I do.

Ghost Rowan puts his hand over mine, the hand that is holding the rowan tree. Ghost Tansy puts her hand over the one that's holding the tansy. I lost a very big part of me when they died. How can anyone ever get back the pieces that their siblings took with them?

"Remember," Grandma says, "when your father gets home, you still have to tell him about that damn tattoo."

That makes all four of us burst into laughter. Six of us, if you count Ghost Tansy and Ghost Rowan.

"I got a tattoo." That's the first thing I blurt out to Dad, not "Hello" or "I missed you." I don't run up to him or jump into his arms, I don't break down crying in the middle of the air-port, and I don't call his name when I spot him from afar. Instead, I say: "I got a tattoo." I blame Grandma for putting it in my head. It must have been the right thing to say, though, because at first Dad's eyes get wide and he looks at me as if I've grown a second head, and then he lets out a big, hearty laugh.

"You're kidding me," he says. The wrinkles under his eyes scrunch up when he smiles, and I can't help but notice that it looks like he got more wrinkles while he was at Sad Camp, even if it was just for a month. Or maybe I just never noticed.

"I'm not kidding."

I show him the smudge. He laughs even harder because he can't tell what it is and has to tilt his head to the side and squint his eyes.

"It looked better before it got infected, I swear."

"It got infected?"

"Oops."

Dad finally closes the distance between us and hugs me in the middle of the busy airport, squishing my face into the buttons on his shirt. Grandma and Grandpa hug him too, and we stand there for a while because we are all that's left of the Summers and we're all afraid that if we break apart, we won't ever fall back together. I don't care how many people are staring at us, wondering what our story is—we stay together for as long as we can.

"Someone get me a cup of coffee," Dad mutters into our necks. "They didn't have coffee there. I *need* it." The thought of Dad without coffee makes me giggle. He used to drink it every single morning and wouldn't say a word to any of us before he had his cup. Mom would always try extra hard to bother him in the morning because he would grumble and mope around and she said it was her goal to get him to laugh before he had his coffee. She accomplished it a couple of times. My parents were so in love.

We get him coffee, and when he takes a sip he makes this face as though he's never tasted anything so good, even though it's just overpriced airport coffee. We make fun of him and none of us say a word about Charles Sanctuary for the Recently Bereaved and it feels like we could be a normal family again one day—not the same normal, but a new kind of normal. Hanna would say that there's no such thing as normal and it's just an idea created by people in power to justify their lifestyles. I've been spending too much time with Hanna; it's like I've got a miniature Hanna in my head. She'd be proud.

Dad's face still looks very sad and sunken. His hair is too long. Mom would have liked it—Mom was always telling him she liked his hair long, but he told her if he grew it long then he would have to use more shampoo and he didn't want to bother. That was actually one of their biggest arguments, at least as far as Tansy and Rowan and I knew.

"Now, take me home," Dad instructs after he finishes his last sip of coffee, downing the entire cup in less than ten minutes. "I need to be home."

Together, we make our way to the car, all standing so close to one another it's as if we're afraid we'll fall apart.

We don't talk much on the way home. Grandpa turns on the car stereo and blasts the classic-rock station because it's Dad's favorite, and Dad sings along the way he used to sing to embarrass Rowan when he dropped us off at school, and I realize I haven't seen him sing like this since before they died. I watch him from the seat beside him and can't help but smile, even though I'm still sort of mad at him for everything.

Stepping into the house with Dad by my side feels so familiar yet simultaneously so foreign. Pumpkin is so excited to see him; I've never seen him that excited—running around in circles and jumping up and down so much I'm afraid he'll hurt his little legs. He probably thought Dad was gone forever like Mom and Rowan and Tansy and is happy to see Dad is back for good. I hope he doesn't get his hopes up—I don't want Pumpkin to think that Mom and Rowan and Tansy will come back too. I bend down and let him lick my face. That makes me feel better.

At home, Grandma and Grandpa make us a special dinner—BBQ ribs and mashed potatoes. Neither of them is very good at cooking, but Dad and I pretend to like it because that's what you do when your grandparents cook you a meal. You smile and shovel it into your mouth, and when they're not looking, you exchange glances and almost burst out laughing because the food really is quite terrible. I'm not sure how a person can mess up mashed potatoes, let alone two people, but somehow Grandma and Grandpa manage to do just that. Even Tansy could cook mashed potatoes. It was actually her specialty for Thanksgivings—the ten-year-old chef.

Grandma asks Dad about his flight and how the process of moving out went. "Smoothly, I'd hope?" she asks. Grandma is being the hard one, the tough one, the one who keeps things moving.

Grandpa asks Dad how he's feeling and if he's tired. He looks like he wants to ask more but doesn't know how to. Grandpa is being the soft one.

I don't ask him anything. I'm not sure which one that makes me—probably just Laurel, who never knows what to say or when to say it and ends up blurting out that she got a tattoo the minute she sees her dad after a month.

"You know," Dad says to me, "you're going to need to explain that tattoo. And then I'm probably obligated to lecture you."

"You better lecture her," mutters Grandma as she waves a spatula around in the air dangerously close to Grandpa's face.

"Only if the story isn't good enough."

I swallow hard because telling him about the tattoo means bringing up Rowan and Tansy, and I'm afraid if I bring them up he'll run out into the forest and never come back. Like if I speak their names I'll remind him of what he ran away to look for in the first place and he'll disappear all over again.

"Well," I say, "I wanted to get plants. You know. A rowan and a tansy. And I did. But then Lyssa and I went swimming afterward and it got infected and they had to remove some of my skin so now it's just a blob."

"You and Lyssa can be idiots."

"We know. Hanna would have stopped us from swimming."

"Hanna would have stopped you from getting the tattoo in the first place," Grandma adds. "Tell him where you got it! Illegally!"

Dad puts his hand up. "Let me guess—Lyssa?"

"Lyssa's ex-foster sister."

"Ah." He looks like he's trying very hard not to laugh, or maybe not to cry; those two reactions look the same right before they happen. "I should probably tell you not to hang out with bad influence Lyssa James anymore."

"But she's my best friend. One of them."

"And a good friend she is, so I'm making an exception."

"She got adopted."

"So, it's official?"

"Yes. I went to court and saw it all happen."

"I sure missed a lot."

"You did."

That's when the air grows thick. It's not when I bring up Tansy and Rowan and my stupid tattoo—it's when we remember that he's been gone nearly all summer and he left me here and I kept living my life without him being around, without any of *them* being around. Dad didn't even bat an eye when I told him what the tattoo was for. That's something he should have teared up over because really, there's a sweet meaning behind it, even though it turned into a smudge. Dad looks confused, like he's just inhaled the air and realizes it's unbreathable.

"And we missed *you* a lot," Grandma says. She's trying to slice through the tension. It doesn't work. I stare at Dad and he stares back at me and instead of seeing him, I see a man who doesn't know what he's doing. Maybe part of growing up is looking at your dad and no longer seeing him as only your dad but also seeing him as a person who hurts and doesn't know what to do sometimes. It's a world-shattering feeling.

"I have something for you," I tell him.

"Oh, yeah?"

"Yeah."

I slide back my chair so it makes a loud squeaking noise against the hardwood (that doesn't slice through the tension, either) and bound up the stairs, two at a time. The pressed maybe-tansy and rowan leaf are in my room. I didn't bring them with me today because I've been trying to get accustomed to not feeling them in my pocket. I didn't even notice they weren't there for most of the day, which makes me feel kind of disappointed in myself. I'm afraid that if I stop feeling attached to those pressed plants then I'll stop feeling attached to Alive Tansy and Alive Rowan. One day, I might forget the sound of Rowan's voice or how many freckles were on Tansy's nose or the way Rowan's hair would curl when it was hot outside.

I miss them. I miss them, I miss them, I miss them.

I clutch the pressed plants to my chest and hold them there like I'm holding on to a stuffed animal or a dog or something that's much more comforting and huggable. I wish Ghost Mom was here to hug me, but Ghost Mom doesn't always show up at the right times. Right now, it's just me. Just me and the pressed plants and my empty bedroom and the sound of my grandparents starting the dishwasher downstairs.

I miss them. I even miss Dad, despite the fact that he's downstairs at the table where I left him, waiting patiently for me to remove the pressed leaves from their place by my heart and bring them to him. I miss them, I miss them, I miss them.

I wish I had been born in the summer. I wish I had bright red hair, like Mom's, so that when I looked in the mirror I could see her again. I wish that my freckles were darker like Tansy's were and I wish that I had Rowan's big smile. I wish that I looked more like them because then Dad would look at me and see them too. My face is made up of equal parts Mom and Dad, but in a way that makes it so I don't look like either of them, and I got my not-quite-red hair from Dad's side so if anything, I look more like him than anyone else. I wish I looked more like Mom.

I stay there in my room for a while thinking about how I wish that I could consume the pressed leaves and become part Tansy and part Rowan. I even text Hanna about it, and Hanna says, "But then where would Laurel go?" I don't have an answer to that. I'm not sure where Laurel is right now, but

I'm starting to get pieces of her back. So, I kiss the pressed plants and then I force myself to stand up and go downstairs and give them to Dad, because I got them for him and he needs them more than I do.

Maybe I'm becoming the hard one—I'm becoming the person who always tries to carry on for other people and be strong, even though I don't want to and I'm really not sure how.

"I found them," I whisper. Dad is sitting at the table with his head in his hands. He glances up at me and frowns. "I found them," I say again. I hold up the plants. "I got these for you. You were looking for them."

Dad doesn't start crying, not immediately. He just frowns at me like he's not sure what I said, as if I've spoken a foreign language. I keep talking. "I found this at the airport. A boy who presses flowers gave it to me. I know it sounds very silly and it might not even be a tansy, but I asked him if I could have it and he gave it to me. And this is from a girl in Scotland. I know, it sounds crazy too, but I found her at the airport and asked her to get one for me and I almost ran away to Scotland but then I realized you have to be eighteen to stay in a hostel so that really wouldn't have gone well. And now I have them and I'm giving them to you because it's what you were looking for."

Dad is starting to tear up. Then he manages to say, "You almost ran away to Scotland?"

"Yes. To find the rowan plant. Well, the tree. But it turns out they're both here, anyways, which makes the whole thing kind of ironic now."

"Running away to Scotland. We'll have to make that the new running away to Peru."

"I don't think it's worthy of replacing Mom's because she actually followed through with running away."

"Laurel. Thank you. My beautiful girl."

"Tansy was your beautiful girl."

Dad shakes his head and says, "Both of you. Mom. Rowan. All beautiful."

"Rowan was a boy."

Dad snorts and says, "You know what I mean."

Then he hugs me. He doesn't take the pressed leaves from my hands—he goes straight into hugging me without even looking at the things I'm handing to him, trying to give to him. He tells me to keep them, that we can both have them, and then he asks, "Can we go somewhere? For a walk?"

I haven't been on a walk with Dad for years, not since we had our old dog, Benny, who came before Pumpkin and was a golden retriever that liked to bark at squirrels so much that Mom refused to walk him because she felt bad for the squirrels. I always walked with Dad. Benny died four years ago, though.

"Yeah, Dad. Let's go for a walk."

Dad tells me about Charles Sanctuary for the Recently Bereaved. He tells me about Jerry, his roommate who lost his wife in a boating accident and would sometimes talk to her in his sleep. He tells me about a woman named Chantel who lost her child to leukemia and was sent to Charles Sanctuary because she hadn't gotten out of bed for seven weeks. He tells me about a mom whose daughter got run over by a car, and a twenty-year-old who lost a friend in a skiing accident.

"That's a lot of recently bereaved people," I mutter.

"Sounds pretty depressing to you, huh?"

"Yes. Very."

"It didn't feel that way—not to me. It made me feel less... alone, you know?"

I nod because I do know. Because all those people at Charles Sanctuary are still living and trying to get better and that makes me think that maybe there is a point to it all. Something keeps us going. Perhaps it's because of the people we lose, or in spite of them. Or maybe it's the people we don't lose, people like Hanna and Lyssa and Grandma and Grandpa and Dad. We're all doing things for other people.

Dad talks for a long time. He tells me about the grieving support groups he was a part of, and how at Charles Sanctuary they called the meetings "Breathing Time" because it was supposed to be a time for them to put down all the heavy things and breathe and listen. "That's a concept I want to work into my novel," Dad says. "How loss can suffocate us, and we need time to breathe."

I still have no idea what Dad's novel is about. When I was seven he told me that it involved space and when I was twelve he said that it was a Western, so I'm not sure what he's going for. But since Mom is gone now, I have to take over being the one who believes in his silly novel.

"That's very poetic," I say.

"I thought so too." He's a literature professor, after all.

He tells me he wants to go back to teaching in the fall. "I think that if I were to take more time off, I'd spiral. And those students, they save me. Even if half of them don't want to be there."

"You're a nerd."

He laughs. He tells me a story about how Jerry the room-mate was a professor of physics and how they would talk about teaching until very late in the night. And sometimes, when Jerry couldn't sleep because he kept seeing his wife in front of him, Dad would recite his favorite passages and Jerry would try to explain string theory to Dad.

"It sounds like sleepaway camp, but for extremely sad adults."

"That just about sums it up."

We walk on a trail that runs by the river behind our house. I make sure to stay on the side near the river. A part of me is still scared Dad is going to try and jump in and drown himself. I wonder if I'll always be afraid of that, just like how I'll always be afraid of trucks driving through a red light or merging lanes on a freeway.

"I missed you, Laurel," he says.

"I missed you too." He puts his arm around me, and I imagine myself slipping away and running from him and yelling at him because he left me. He can't just come back and tell me he missed me. I try to bite my tongue but a few of the words tumble out of my mouth: "If you missed me, why did you leave me?"

Dad tenses up but doesn't remove his arm from around me. I want to punch him in the face. I also want to hug him and never let him go and take him home and make sure he never jumps into a river or off a cliff.

"Because I think…I think that if I didn't go there I wouldn't be *here*. And then I wouldn't be able to miss you, and I think I needed to miss you."

"So, either way you would have left me."

"I didn't leave you."

"You did!" I slide out from his arms and turn to face him. "You left me in that bush! And then you took those pills and you left me to go to Kentucky! And I was all by myself! Because you left me!"

The words don't break him into a million pieces like I expect them to. I stand with my back toward the water, and a part of me is prepared to throw myself at Dad to stop him from jumping, but he doesn't break this time. He just looks at me with eyes that scream regret, and a single tear falls down his cheek. I'm the one breaking into a million pieces. My soul is scattered in fragments all over this riverbank.

"Laurel," he says. His voice is soft and quiet, like Grandpa's. "Your mother and I never wanted you to worry."

"What is that supposed to mean?"

"I should have told you. I've been very sad for a long time. Depressed. I'm depressed. And without them…without them I guess it just pushed me to a very dark place."

"And then you left me."

"I didn't leave you."

"You did! In that bush!"

He closes his eyes tightly like he's trying very hard not to cry. It's out of character. Dad cries easily. Both he and Mom were always like that. Rowan hated it.

"I'm sorry," he says.

I don't say anything back.

"I was in a dark place."

"We're all in a dark place."

"I'm sick. I've been sick for a long time. I never wanted you to worry. I didn't think—I didn't think it would get that bad. Ever. I was on medication, it was under control. But then we lost…your mom, and your brother and sister, and… it brought me there. I hadn't been there since I was fifteen, Laurel."

"I'm fifteen right now. And I needed you right now."

"I'm here. I'm here now."

"You're not allowed to leave me again."

"I'll never leave you. I just had to go away to get better. I'm taking antidepressants, a stronger dosage than before, and I think it will help, and I'll go to therapy and Grandma and Grandpa will be here."

"I'm going to therapy."

"That's right."

"Her name is Shannon. I like her. If she wasn't my therapist I would be friends with her. Is that a weird thing to say?"

Dad smiles. His smile makes more tears run down his cheeks, pressing them out of his eyes and forcing them onto his face. "I sure did miss a lot."

"You did."

"I'm sorry."

"I know."

"I really am."

We keep walking. I see a leaf fall in front of me. It's only August, too early for leaves to be falling, but I guess fall is coming early this year. I stop and look at the river while Dad stands next to me.

"I'm not going to say it's OK," I tell him. "But I get it. Sort of. Not entirely. I don't get the part about you leaving me in the laurel bush. I get the part about missing them. That's why I found the rowan and the tansy for you."

"Not just for me. For both of us. They were ours, Laurel, not just mine."

"But you're sadder."

"I don't think that's true. Besides, sadness isn't a competition."

Maybe Dad and I will never be the same again and maybe that's OK, because we'll create a new normal and I'll get mad at him for leaving me sometimes and he'll apologize a lot and maybe we'll never get over it, but we'll move on, somehow. It doesn't have to be in a bad way, because Rowan and Tansy and Mom still live in us, in the garden and in my smudged tattoo and in the way Lyssa talks about astrology.

"I want to do something," Dad says.

"What?"

He takes us down the trail and stops to stare at the ground. A laurel bush. A stupid, stupid laurel bush. Then he reaches into his pocket and pulls out a bag of what looks like dirt, but I know better. I've already seen the ashes of three people I love.

"So that they'll live in you," he tells me. He opens the bag and nods for me to reach in. I grab onto the dust and think about how it's Mom and Rowan and Tansy all ground up into dirt, which is very odd. It's weird that humans do this. Why do we turn people to ashes? These ashes aren't even all of them because parts of them were scattered over the road and smashed and probably dried up and evaporated or got washed away with the rain. I'll always be missing something, like they'll always be missing somewhere.

I sprinkle a pinch of the dust onto the laurel bush and it disappears into the dirt. We both stand there, looking at the bush, me thinking about the time I sat in one and Dad left me. Dad is rocking back and forth on his heels like he's waiting for something spectacular to happen, as if Mom and Rowan and Tansy will rise from the ashes and dance with us in the forest. They don't.

"My plant is the most boring," I say.

"Everyone thinks they're the most boring."

I turn to him and he turns to me and looks at me hard, like he's taking in everything, from my uneven freckles to my eyes that are somewhere between Mom's brown and his blue to my hair that is only red when it's hit with the right kind of sunlight.

"First of all," I say, "you got that saying from Grandpa."

"I did."

"Second of all, I said the bush was boring, not me. So, the saying doesn't apply because there is a distinction. And third, the bush is boring because it's everywhere here and not hard to find, unlike the rowan trees that grow in Scotland and, apparently, in some places here and have bright red berries and long branches. Or the tansy that we had to drive up to the pass to find that is bright yellow and beautiful, even though a boy at a flower shop said it's technically a weed."

Dad shakes his head. "But Laurel," he says, "isn't that just the thing? Isn't it beautiful because it's everywhere?"

"That's why it's not beautiful. Also, I don't have Mom's red hair. So, I'm not really related to Mom, at least I don't feel like I am."

"Those two things don't seem related."

"They feel related."

"Ah."

"And I really wish I did have redder hair because then I'd look like Mom or Rowan or Tansy."

"You're beautiful, Laurel."

"I'm boring."

"We're all boring. But we still love each other."

"Mom wasn't boring."

"She thought she was, sometimes."

"Really?"

"Of course."

Dad bends down and rips off a leaf from the laurel bush. He holds it up to my face and says, "Just because something is everywhere doesn't mean it's less beautiful." I feel myself blush even though it's just a silly, boring leaf, and Dad smiles at me. "Have I ever told you about the time Mom picked out your name?"

He tells me that when Mom found out she was pregnant with a girl, she refused to name me after a flower, because girls were always named after flowers, and she wanted to name me after a plant. She spent months pointing to shrubs and leaves and asking my dad, "What's that one called?" Dad would look up the names of all the plants she pointed to and, eventually, she came across a laurel bush and pointed and asked my dad.

"That's a laurel bush," Dad told her.

And Mom exclaimed, "Laurel! That's it!" The story makes me miss Mom.

I don't think we'll ever be whole again without Mom and Rowan and Tansy. Instead, we'll be something new entirely, but we'll keep the rowan tree and the tansy flower pressed like bookmarks in our lives. I wish Mom was named after a plant too. There isn't a flower I can press for the name Marlene.

Dad and I are both crying now, except this time the tears feel lighter and happier and less angry. I don't know if I'm still angry at him—I haven't decided yet. He hands me the laurel leaf and says, "We'll press this one, too," which makes me feel warm inside because then we can line it up next to the may-be-tansy and the rowan leaf and the Summers siblings will be complete, in pressed-plant form at least.

A big part of me is still kind of upset that I was named after the bush that is everywhere—even though Tansy and Rowan are dead I'm still envious of them, which feels very wrong. But maybe it's OK because Mom chose the name for me and I really do miss her. Dad and I are the ones left to carry her and keep her alive. Grandma and Grandpa and Hanna and Lyssa help us carry the weight, but it's really up to us and the laurel bushes that hold her ashes. They're every-where. She's everywhere. I'm everywhere.

It's the morning of the first day of school and I'm sitting across from Shannon, a cup of coffee warming my hands and my backpack at my feet.

"It's the first day, huh?"

I nod.

"How are things going with your dad?"

"Fine enough," I tell her, which is the truth. They're not perfect—everything changed with the accident, including my trust in Dad, but things are better than they were because he's back now for good. Some days he seems so distant, like he's floating around in space, and I become afraid he'll get bad again and have to go away. But it passes, and we keep going. Grandma and Grandpa help with that, sneaking in with their poorly cooked meals and their offers to drive me places, acting as pseudo-parents when Dad can't. But this morning was good because Dad had a smile on his face and cooked me pancakes for the first day of school and offered to drive me to therapy early in the morning before dropping me off at the high school. He's sitting outside right now, reading his book in the car and sipping on his morning tea.

"And are you OK with that?" Shannon asks me.

"Yeah," I tell her. I am OK with it. I'm OK with things being just OK. Because at least they're not terrible-rock-bottom anymore.

"Big day today," she says. We scheduled the appointment for this morning because she was worried it would be hard for me, that I might need to talk to someone before returning to school. But surprisingly, I feel calm, like I can handle it. The ghosts aren't in my head anymore, not as much, but I still feel them. Mom and Rowan and Tansy are all around me, but they've stopped yelling at me and clouding my thoughts. They're settled, at least for now, and I think Lyssa may have been onto something when she said that ghosts only appear when they have a message for you.

"I'll be OK," I reassure her. I don't know that I'll be good or bad, but I'll be somewhere in between. I'll go to school and I'll get bored in class and maybe I'll get upset when I think about how it would have been Rowan's senior year, or Tansy's first day of middle school, but I'll make it through the day and I'll come home and I'll see Dad and Grandma and Grandpa.

"Laurel?" Shannon says, a sly smile on her face as I begin to gather my things, getting ready to leave.

"Yeah?"

"We talked about a couple of the items on The List."

"Oh, yeah?"

"We talked about your dad, going to school, your mom and siblings..."

She's smiling at me, and I can't help but smile back.

"Yeah, well, maybe The List wasn't the best coping mechanism I've ever had." I grin and swing my bag over my shoulder. "See what I did there? My coping mechanisms. That was number 2. I'm really breaking all the rules today!"

She laughs and opens the door for me. "Take care of yourself today at school. Feel free to call the office if there's anything you need."

"Will do."

An hour later, I'm standing a block away from the front steps of my school. Early-September leaves are beginning to fall, oranges and reds mixed in with the dark green laurel leaves that are always there, no matter the season. I watch as kids file through the doors like sardines with backpacks of all different colors and the cheerleaders stand in the entrance welcoming us back to school with pom-poms and huge smiles on their faces. "I hate cheerleaders," Lyssa mumbles, rolling her eyes beside me.

"I'm pretty sure everyone hates cheerleaders," Hanna replies.

"Everyone that's not a cheerleader," I add.

"Honestly, I think cheerleaders also hate other cheerleaders," Lyssa says. That makes all three of us laugh. They put their arms around me and Hanna says, "OK, everyone, take a deep breath." We all exhale loudly and Lyssa mutters, "Our last breath of fresh air before we enter hell."

We can't stop giggling. Even though Hanna is very good at school, she still hates it like the rest of us. I don't know of a teenager who doesn't hate high school. Teenagers who like high school are definitely a myth. I'm sure of it.

"You OK?" Hanna asks me. I think about Rowan, envision him sauntering in through the door like he owns the place. I think about Tansy nervously hugging me before bouncing over to her own school down the street. Before this summer, that would have been normal, but normal is gone. We've thrown that out the window.

"Not really," I tell Hanna, "but I'm not crying, so I think I'm OK enough to go inside."

"Not crying is always the goal," Lyssa says while elbowing me in the ribs.

"If you keep hitting me like that, I'm going to start crying."

We laugh, because sometimes that's all you can do. We walk arm in arm toward the school building. I know when everyone sees me, they're going to see the girl with the dead family, instead of just the girl who was named after a bush.

And I'll carry on like Grandma and I'll probably cry in the school hallways like Grandpa. And I'll go home each day and see them, because Grandma and Grandpa have decided to move in with us, for a while. Each night, I'll walk Pumpkin with Dad and we'll talk, and each day the tension will erode between us until eventually, we're OK again.

And maybe one day I'll stop being the girl with the dead family. Not in the sense that I'll forget about them, or that anyone else will forget about them, but in the sense that I'll carry them with me and they'll be a part of me that doesn't feel so sad and heavy but feels right. And I'll be Laurel. Just Laurel.

When I get home from school, Dad says he has a surprise for me. He has this goofy grin on his face, and Grandma and Grandpa put a blindfold over my eyes and guide me through the house like it's a maze until we reach a door that leads outside. "OK, open," Dad directs.

In the side yard, despite the early signs of fall's arrival, Mom's garden is in full bloom.

DISCUSSION GUIDE

1. Throughout the novel, characters react to grief in different ways. How does each character react, and what does this say about the way grief affects people? Which character reminds you the most of yourself? How has your own experience with grief shifted your relationships?

2. Lyssa and Hanna both respond to Laurel's grief in vastly different ways—Lyssa tends to distract Laurel, while Hanna wants to busy herself and help. In what ways would you support a friend in mourning?

3. Think about the ways that Laurel and her dad are impacted by the loss of their family. In what ways do they express their grief? How do their individual responses to their loss impact their relationship with one another?

4. How does Laurel's understanding of her dad's grief give her insight into him as a person?

5. Do you think Laurel ever forgave the truck driver? Why or why not? Would you forgive the truck driver?

6. Laurel creates a "list of things not to talk about." While Hanna chastises Laurel for avoiding talking about her feelings, Laurel's therapist listens to and respects The List. Why is this significant for Laurel, and why do you think Laurel finally decides she's ready to breach the subjects on The List?

7. How does Laurel's perspective of her namesake shift throughout the novel?

8. How has your own mental health impacted your relationships with others and yourself?

9. Laurel clings to the symbols of her siblings to ground herself and help her father cope. How can symbols like music, literature, and other art forms offer a sense of comfort for you?

10. For people who've lost loved ones, birthdays and other important dates can be really difficult. How did Laurel honor her siblings and her mom's memory? How do you honor the loved ones you've lost?

HELP LINES

Crisis Text Line: Visit www.crisistextline.org/ for free, 24/7 support for those in crisis. Text "START" to 741-741 from anywhere in the US to text with a trained Crisis Counselor.

List of International Suicide Hotlines: Visit www.suicide.org/international-suicide-hotlines.html Call: 1-800-784-2433

Love is Respect: Visit www.loveisrespect.org/. Love is Respect's purpose is to engage, educate and empower young people to prevent and end abusive relationships. Text "LOVEIS" to 22522 or call 1-866-331-9474 to talk with a peer advocate to prevent and end abusive relationships.

National Suicide Prevention Lifeline: Visit www.suicide-preventionlifeline.org/ or call 1-800-273-TALK (8255).

Therapy Den: an online community of mental health professionals seeking to make the experience of finding a therapist easy. https://www.therapyden.com/

The Trevor Project: Visit https://www.thetrevorproject.org/ The Trevor Project is the leading national organization providing crisis intervention and suicide prevention services to lesbian, gay, bisexual, transgender, queer & questioning (LGBTQ) young people under 25. Call: 1-866-488-7386

Acknowledgments

I wrote this book in a fury. It was an idea that came to me fully formed, the characters clear as crystal in my mind. I wrote it over the course of three months, which is quite possibly the fastest I've ever written a novel. It's thanks to so many people in my life that I didn't stop there—that this book became what it did, that it grew in ways that felt meaningful and authentic.

First and foremost, I'd like to thank my team at Ooligan Press. Their unwavering support and belief in Laurel's story fueled me during long nights of editing.

I'd also like to thank all my lifelong cheerleaders. Manasa—thank you for being the first to read this story, for your witty comments on the side of my manuscript document and of course, for being my first ever writing partner. Michael—thank you for bringing me tea and water and food while I write furiously, and listening to my ideas with open ears. Mary K, Mary D, Grace, and Erica—thank you for cheering me on via group texts and heartfelt Instagram messages when it comes to all my writing-related worries! And there are so many others too who have supported my writing along the way. You all know who you are, and thank you.

Last but not least, thank you to my family—Mom, Dad, Sammie, and all the dogs. You've given me enough inspiration for quirky family dynamics to last a lifetime.

About the Author

Erin Moynihan is a writer from Seattle, Washington, where she spends many rainy days typing away in coffee shops. She hails from a background in social work, elements of which she brings to her writing. Her editorial work has appeared in outlets such as HuffPost, BuzzFeed, The Mighty, and various others. She's passionate about breaking the stigma around mental health and centering young female voices. When she's not working, she's likely spending time cuddling with her dog or adventuring around the Pacific Northwest.

You can see what she's up to at www.erinmoynihan.com.

Ooligan Press

Ooligan Press is a student-run publishing house rooted in the rich literary culture of the Pacific Northwest. Founded in 2001 as part of Portland State University's Department of English, Ooligan is dedicated to the art and craft of publishing. Students pursuing master's degrees in book publishing staff the press in an apprenticeship program under the guidance of a core faculty of publishing professionals.

Project Managers
Tia Sprague
Grace Hansen

Acquisitions
Ari Mathae
Taylor Thompson
Des Hewson
Kim Scofield

Editing
Madison Schultz
Melinda
 Crouchley
Emma Wolf
Olivia Rollins

Design
Denise
 Morales Soto
Morgan Ramsey

Digital
Megan Crayne
Christopher Leal

Marketing
Sydnee Chesley
Hannah
 Boettcher

Social Media
Faith Muñoz
Alix Martinez

Book Production
McKenna Green
Corey Talbott
Kali Carryl
Alexandria
 Gonzales
Ivy Knight
Ruth Robertson

Sean Paul Lavine
Jennifer Ladwig
Courtney Young
Michael
 Shymanski
Vivian Nguyen
Erica Wright
Rosina Miranda
Mary Williams
Kaitlyn Shehee
Bailey Potter
Hannah
 Boettcher
Giacomo Ranieri
Anastacia Ferry
Kendra Ferguson